THE LANGUAGE OF GRACE

FAITH, FAMILY & FRIENDS

THE LANGUAGE OF GRACE

FAITH, FAMILY & FRIENDS

GRACE GALTON

A Parisian Book
Published by Parisian Press

© 2005 Grace Galton
All rights reserved.

Printed in The United States of America

7 6 5 4 3 2 1

First Hardcover printing: December 2005

Publisher Cataloging-in-Publication Data
Galton, Grace
The Language of Grace: Faith, Family and Friends / Grace Galton
        p.   cm.
ISBN 1-4116-6336-5
1. Galton, Grace.   2. Religion—United States—Autobiography   3. Grief and healing—United States—Autobiography   4. Women Authors, American—Family Relationships   5. Women Authors, American—Memoir   I. Title

ISBN and distribution provided by Lulu Press, 3131 RDU Center Dr., Suite 210, Morrisville, NC 27560. Telephone 919-459-5858.

Cover and book design by Grace Galton and Jef Clarke
Cover photography by Mark Galton and Jef Clarke
Montage design by Todd Wawrychuk

For Steve,

my treasured Galtie, faithful friend,
sagacious husband, shining star,
caretaker of memories…

ACKNOWLEDGMENTS

This book would never exist apart from my dear friends, Jef and Holly Clarke. At a pivotal point in time, we met on life's path and they agreed to follow my family's unfolding story. Gently, but with great humor, they held on to the bag of shattered pieces until we could begin to reassemble them.

I thank my brothers for stepping in and offering their big shoulders at the times when I needed family the most.

Thank you, Maureen Lucas, for inviting me to join you on the great adventure of writing. It was kind of you to drive me to class in your red Miata, which was actually a Porsche.

Thank you, Donna Mungen—you have inspired me with your sharp, perceptive insights, and suggestions as a writing teacher.

Thank you, Nayiri and Susan Partamian—I come into your beautiful shop with expectations always. People can never buy what you provide, but your teacups have overflowed with compassion, and our goblets have tinkled and resonated with marital hope and harmony.

Thank you, Bob Lucas, for sharing the vision and for renovating the second Shepherd's Home in Kenya.

Thank you, Kay and John Alsip—for your chili recipe and for sharing your home, as well as your journal. I send you continued hugs for forty-three years of friendship and encouragement.

Thank you, Cec and Dan Regis—you pray for our family every day. You keep on giving to the whole world, and I thank you for your model of daily prayer, hospitality, and constant support.

Thank you, Margot Webb-Foltz for spiritual guidance, a thousand laughs, the deck experiences, and the "cloth that binds."

Thank you, my patient husband, Steve, who taught me how to turn on the computer and listened attentively as every word spilled forth.

And thank you, dear Mark, for your Thanksgiving sunset—the last picture you took of this life graces the cover of my own earthly journey.

CONTENTS

PREFACE

I wrote this memoir, which spans six decades, while walking on a healing path. I used to think that being a "good enough" woman meant being perfect in the eyes of others. In my writing, I recalled key events in my childhood and was reminded that along with acquiring certain skills, one needs also a sense of humor and the compassion to forgive oneself for all the mistakes we make. Like the magical language I once practiced, I have changed and grown.

I present this book as a gift to my husband and friends and as a legacy to my children. I wrote it with love and honesty, and hope not to offend anyone mentioned—or not mentioned—but these are my words as they hit the page. I express my view of my own life without censoring and revising my words until they are no longer my own.

Over these many years, I have been touched deeply by glimpsing God in everything. I feel God's presence in the radiance of the sunset, the squeezing of a baby's hand, and the yellow birds that keep watch in my yard. I hope to remind my family and friends to love not only their human neighbors, but to love all the precious life around them.

Living a life of wisdom is not about emphasizing religious doctrines. Loving deeply means that you respond to others with your whole heart and with your actions. I want to share my belief that I have been sustained by a sacred mystery way beyond myself that constantly heals and calls me into new life.

PROLOGUE:
THE SHATTERING

I NEVER WEAR SWEAT PANTS and I don't perspire. I wouldn't be caught dead in sweats. It was like all the times my mother had warned me to always wear clean white underwear.

"You just never know when you'll be in an accident. You don't want to be wearing soiled underpants," she cautioned me years ago.

Clutching a peach-colored pot containing a houseplant I had just watered in the sink amidst the dirty cereal bowls, my attention focused on the kitchen clock. Darn it! I was late for an appointment at my church and had not yet showered. Immediately, I rushed across the kitchen into the hallway. Our bedroom and bath were situated down that hall. There it happened.

Plunging downward, violently into a black abyss, I tumbled headfirst. Confusion. Terror. I wondered, *What is happening to me? Am I dying? Will God hold on to me? Is this the end?*

Moments later, the plumber reported the scream he heard from within the house.

"Oh, ugh…help me…please…somebody come," I begged.

"Lady, what's going on here?" the plumber responded. "Just a second…I'm coming," he yelled.

My body felt as though it had been hurled into the air without my brain attached. During the fall, I couldn't grab onto anything. There was no rail to break the fall. The free fall struck me with such forceful fear and fright. *Was this the end?* Darkness engulfed me and I heard the thud of my body smack against the cement. I was prepared to die, and I called out, "God, help me!" Fragments of the shattered plant pot smashed around me. Everything became still. And then there was only blackness—merciful unconsciousness.

"Lady, wake up…wake up. You had a bad fall. Don't move yet. We have to stabilize your neck," the paramedic spoke to me as he cradled my head in his hands. "Don't move. Remain perfectly still."

These instructions made no sense to me as my arms and legs were twisted behind my back. A blood pressure cuff was placed on my arm. Immediately, an oxygen tube was inserted in my nose. Someone was bending over my badly bruised body. I could feel a rising lump on my forehead. Sucking in a breath hurt.

"What happened to me? Where am I? Am I still alive?"

All these questions I tried to ask. "Why am I here? Where is Steve?"

Voices—so many voices—everyone was talking and babbling. Nothing made any sense. Where was I? Why couldn't I remember? Gradually came the awareness of great discomfort. Within moments came a blissful silence.

Mercifully, I was conscious of nothing. The force of the concussion knocked me out for a minute.

"Lady, lady, who shall we call? Give us a number!"

"Call Jan, my friend. Jan Roberts, call her," I responded.

"What's her telephone number?"

"I don't know. My head hurts." I focused then managed to mumble some of the number.

"No, lady. Give us the entire number."

Eventually, the contractor dialed the number I had given him and notified my friend, Jan. Stunned, she rushed back to my house. Chaos and bedlam dominated the scene. I recall absolute craziness. Sirens wailed down the street. Ambulance attendants arrived. Firemen gazed down into the basement hole where I lay. I was told to lie perfectly still.

"We have to get a stretcher down there to you. We aren't sure if you have a neck or back injury. Take it easy," they kept saying.

Later, paramedics told me they worked forty-five minutes to lower the stretcher down to where they could reach me. Warned not to move, I lay unable to comprehend the seriousness of this abrupt descent. Nor was I able to imagine what might possibly be the explanation for the fall. All I could remember was being on my way to the bathroom. Eventually, the stretcher was lifted up the ladder stairs. I was carried up to the hallway landing and I was whisked away outside to the waiting ambulance.

First, I noticed in my hazy state that the street was lined with fire trucks. In that embarrassing moment, I realized that I had not showered and was wearing… sweat pants. Suddenly, I felt like I was eight years old and wearing soiled underpants.

Neighbors were mingling and talking to the contractor and the plumber. "What happened? Who is it? How did she fall?" Quickly, I saw the concerned faces of my friend, Jan and my husband, Steve. Steve was pushing his way past the paramedics toward me. He bent down and kissed me "Honey, what happened?" he asked in a worried voice.

"Steve, I was just with her about an hour ago," Jan explained calmly. "We walked around the Rose Bowl. Since it is such a gorgeous morning, we sat outside on your patio and had a cup of coffee. Then, I needed to get home. This must have happened right after I left."

"Grace, Grace, it's me. I'm here now. They said you fell. It's okay. I'm here. We're going to the hospital now," Steve tried to reassure me. His presence alone makes me feel secure when I am injured. Nonetheless, he looked apprehensive.

Once again, the sirens began to blare. In the emergency room, staff rushed around inserting needles and performing tests. Hours blurred into a long stretch of confusion. There were CAT scans and doctors and nurses. Later came MRI's and neurologists and needles.

"Just one more procedure," the doctor urged.

"No more!" I begged. I was confused and had throbbing pain. By now, my body yearned for rest. "Please, just leave me alone," I pleaded.

My head ached as though it had been placed into a vise and squeezed. Each time I took a breath, there was a stabbing sensation in my chest. Distress and anxiety diminished after seeing that Mark, our twenty-seven year-old son and his seventeen year-old sister, Lissy had arrived to be a comfort. Little did we know then, that only six short years later, Steve, Lissy and I would be offering consoling care to Mark.

Once the pain medication began to take effect, we began to sift through the events of the morning. That season, our house was undergoing a major remodeling project. A portion of our floor plan includes a back hallway with oak wood flooring. A heavy trap door is set into the floor. When the door is opened, a flight of rickety stairs descends twelve feet down to a small basement area.

In a seven foot square space is contained a hot water heater, boxes of old college textbooks, some moldy French books, a broken train set, and a furnace. We always inform anybody in the house whenever the trap door is lifted due to the danger.

"Never open this door or venture down those stairs unless someone is with you to prop up the door with this pole. It is very unsafe. Do you hear me? Never leave the door open. Anyone could fall and kill himself," I admonished all my children. No one ventures down there unless we smell a rotting animal corpse or need to repair the old furnace.

That morning, the plumber had been working down in the basement when the electricity suddenly cut off. He had climbed the stairs and disappeared outside the house to trip the breaker. In his haste, he had forgotten to close the heavy door. Without electricity, the hallway was enclosed in absolute blackness. Within those few minutes, I had returned from a walk with Jan, shared a coffee on the back patio and said goodbye. As I had watered a plant that looked wilted on the kitchen sink, I noticed my lateness for the appointment and I began to run through the house to the bathroom shower that I never reached.

My two ribs were broken and I sustained a concussion. Head injuries are serious and some do not heal with time—in fact, some get much worse. Headaches have plagued me now for nine years since the fall, and I worry for the future state of my mind. For many months, I chose another route to the bathroom.

Traumas produce disbelief and shock and the emotional experience of the descent has had an adverse and lasting psychological impact. This is the point in time where I choose to reveal my life story. I begin my memoirs with a certain humility realizing that portions of my memory were lost in that ordeal.

Something else was signified to me in that frightening event which seems equally alarming: I think I began to lose my firm footing. I don't mean to say that I can't keep my balance down a flight of stairs or walk without stumbling; rather, I began to *fall into a pattern* of not remembering. Formerly, I prided myself on my memory for detail.

My mother had been slipping away for years into a world of mental estrangement and was seriously impaired with Alzheimer's disease. One of the great frustrations of caring for aging parents is watching one's parent descend into unknowingness. Mother eventually ceased talking. Her illness was so debilitating that she could only ask, "Where's Walter?" Towards the end of her eleven-year illness, she just babbled nonsense.

After her death three years ago, I came to an inner peace about my mother. Over the years, much has happened inside me to soften the hardness and bitterness I felt towards her. Mother was attempting to reach out and make a connection, but she was unsuccessful in making those intimate connections. In her mind, she saw the homemade pies and cakes she served as an offering of herself to me. How severely I judged her inadequacy to engage in an authentic emotional dialogue.

In the nursing home, I began to view her as an old woman whom God loves and tentatively held her hand and embraced her. It was amazing how she softened and wept quietly when I bade her goodbye. In that moment, a remarkable gift of understanding came to both of us. It was not until my last trip home to visit her that I reached a sincere forgiveness.

Too many terrible losses have impacted our family's lives over these past nine years since the accident. We are still reeling from disorientation and pain. Privately at times, I have begun to convince myself that much of the accuracy of my memory is deteriorating, and in another year or so, I may not even remember who I am. Will I follow my mother's faltering footsteps into an unbearable demise? Will my death be peaceful? Will my daughter come to my side and listen as I did to my mother? For hours at the onset of her dementia, I tape recorded a living history of her life back three generations. Following her memorial service, I gave this CD to each of my three brothers.

So whenever I hear someone say, "My mind went blank," I shudder. Having a blank mind is one thing, but having a mind full of ideas and feelings to express—and not being able to express them— that is my biggest fear. Losing my ability to communicate—the gift of *language*— for me would be the ultimate disgrace.

I have learned many languages in life; that is, many different ways to express and communicate. I have practiced and lived the *languages* of love, adolescence, independence, grief, and others. These are strange worlds of intricate complexities—they each take a lifetime to truly understand what they are saying, and to discover your own true voice. Faith might be the hardest language of all; it has no rules and one must often work in dim light to understand its evolving message.

After my fall, I began to change. This happened subtly and I tried to keep my fear within myself. I am going to talk about my life now while I still am able to say what appears to be of significance. These reflections are my legacy to my family and friends.

So in this book, I offer you the material of my life and what I observe about how God and I have woven it all together. The texture of the fabric is not seamless. The top of the cloth is classic organdy and rich silk. But I offer you the burlap underside of the quilt with all the scraggly threads hanging out and holes where the stitching has come unraveled.

I am coming to a peaceful sense of the life I know instead of living the illusion of *happily ever after*. My faith stitches my life together and reminds me that I expect to be eternally connected with those dear ones I so love and so miss.

I

MY MAGICAL LANGUAGE: EARLY CHILDHOOD

SNAPSHOTS IN THE PINK baby book called *Our Baby's First Seven Years* depict a small, blond girl usually holding a purse in one hand, wearing a pique bonnet, white sandals, and sometimes waving. I am astonished to notice that I had sent out a birth announcement for my daughter that was identical to the one my mother sent out for me—same card stock, same pink trim, same pink satin ribbon adorning my official name.

My parents both believed that a child's behavior reflects to some extent the consistency and type of training given. "Children must be taught emotional control," my mother wrote. She listed my character traits in my baby book, and most were quite positive: happy, affectionate, sociable, willful, confident, sensitive, and disorderly.

However, there was a special note in the book where she described me as being "not tractable," and she perceived this to be a negative quality. *The Merriam-Webster Unabridged Dictionary* clearly describes tractability as a quality in a person who is *easily managed, controlled, docile, compliant and malleable.* That's not me. At no time have those been descriptors of my behavior or the genetic component I inherited. *C'est la vie que J'ai été donnée.* It's true. This is the one precious life I have been given. You must be true to yourself, and that's not a negative quality.

While reflecting on the idea of penning a personal memoir, I began to think about a pattern that has been pervasive over my entire lifetime. A theme has been woven through the texture of my life, which I would describe as acquiring the nuances of listening to and speaking various languages. In this portion of remembering what glimmers or stands out in my own recollection, I want to focus on a specific time frame in this chapter about key events that occurred between three and eight years of age.

Part of what inspired my childhood was the gaining through my own efforts, the acquisition of my magic language, which I used with some fluency during the ages of seven and eight. Magic language was the fabrication of an interior fantasy world. My parents both subscribed to a fundamentalist theology. They had inherited a belief that the scripture is inerrant and central to any other sacrament.

Although a Baptist, I was innately a Jewish person. Mother was unaware of this religious preference so it was not included in the pink baby book. Most of the neighborhood in which we lived on the south side of Chicago was composed of people whose surnames ended with the suffix, "stein."

Freda Schwartz, a lively, petite, dark haired neighbor could be seen through our kitchen window scurrying about her breakfast nook. Frequently, I was invited over there, as my mother was bedridden due to a complicated pregnancy and the threat of a miscarriage. I simply do not remember my mother as displaying much emotional warmth.

When my mother was thirteen, her older brother had died, and I don't think she ever acquired the skills of intimacy or trust with others.

Among Freda's blessed actions were her nurturing skills. When anyone was hurt, she applied a liquid red Mercurochrome ointment to the skinned elbows and knees of children. It was to her kitchen that I limped after bicycle accidents and injured feelings. Seldom were any children allowed into her parlor because that was a formal space. White couches were covered in a transparent plastic material. In the bathroom over the medicine cabinet hung a bluish colored ultra violet lamp, a modern day miracle treatment that was supposed to cure measles, polio, and other assorted illnesses. We were all terrified of polio and knew of a woman who lay in an iron lung.

Larry Schwarz, her husband was a burley man who wore thick eyeglasses and drove a Buick car. On occasion, especially during the high holy days, he brought groceries to our home from the delicatessen that he owned. Jewish food tasted mysterious and exotic to a little girl raised on ham and scalloped potatoes.

Matzo ball soup and tuna fish casserole with peas were two of the delicacies Freda prepared. Tapioca pudding was another delight. I could see through the window five feet away that Freda wet mopped her kitchen floor every night. On hot, muggy summer afternoons, we climbed the branches of her apple tree and waited for the Good Humor man to drive his truck down the alley. Then we rushed in our house to beg a nickel for an ice cream treat.

This seventh year of my life became the crisis point of my budding faith and language development. Already, I had been speaking the magic language three years. Something new began to creep into my desire and awareness. I decided to act Jewish too.

My parents, however, viewed my tenacity to become a Jew as a betrayal of my Baptist roots. Above all else, I yearned to speak Yiddish fluently. Visions grow and I practiced my make-believe Yiddish playing outside in the neighborhood. I prattled on and on in my language with the rising intonations reserved for any Jewish man wearing a small black beanie on his head. I always made sure that I was loud enough so that people would recognize that I was a foreigner—and was kin to a Jewish heritage.

Then at night in my bed, I remember feeling a sort of loneliness. A great comfort was looking at the bed stand on which stood a night light which was a white plastic Jesus figure to whom I confessed my secret longing to be Jewish. Something mystical happened, I am convinced. That night light became a symbol of great comfort to me and illumined not only my bedroom but also my heart. I would experience the blessing of Jesus in my evening prayers.

Obeying rules was a key principle in my upbringing. Parameters were clearly delineated where I could walk or play. My older brother Robert and I were permitted to cross the alley from our house and walk to Jeffrey Avenue where my father descended the bus each workday at 5: 50 pm. My dad is a cheerful man and I wanted him to be proud of me. Going to the bus stop, for me, became an intimate experience in admiring my father. I always remember that I was proud of his ability to engage people in conversation and become involved in what seemed to be a relevant and topical discourse. Later I realized that he just liked to hear himself talk.

So it became a ritual to pass the Davis' house with their grown-up Catholic children and gigantic Dahlia garden, our own vegetable garden and rhubarb patch, and on to Bennett and Euclid Avenues past the three story brick flats with the rear porches and fire escapes. These walks to greet my Dad provided ample opportunities to speak my language totally unrestrained.

Neighbors gazed at my blond blue-eyed appearance and gaped over my startling vocabulary. My brother and I took turns pulling each other in the red "flyer" wagon, yet he never spoke to the neighbors. Pretending to speak Yiddish never earned me a well-deserved and coveted place in Hebrew school. I only got to attend once with Freddy Schwartz.

Instead, on Sundays, which was our Sabbath day of rest, our family took a streetcar down 87th Street west a couple miles. Pulling on the cord above the green bus seats indicated to the bus driver that we had arrived at our destination. The four of us family members hiked two blocks to Lorimer Memorial Baptist Church. Services were long and I daydreamed through the sermons.

I often wondered if Jesus was waiting for me beyond the puffy cumulus clouds to reassure me that He loved my robust singing. On those summer Sundays when we returned home on the same dusty streetcar, we ate an enormous roast beef and potato Sunday dinner, complete with an assortment of vegetables from my dad's Victory Garden. No one succeeded in forcing me to eat the tomatoes but I did savor Swiss chard. Our grandparents had a new green 1949 Packard, and on occasion they joined us for those Sunday afternoons.

I was very alert to rhythm and remember my grandparents calling attention to many rhythms including the sound of surf, woodpeckers in the trees, the sounds of sawing tree branches, and even the gentle rustle of the wind blowing through the oak trees. Dancing amused me and I loved listening to the Firestone Hour on the radio each Sunday evening because I believed the actual voices were little musicians living inside the upright radio.

My grandfather did not attend church. He was a tall, thin man who played golf, smoked cigarettes, and listened to his large collection of New Orleans jazz records. My grandmother expressed concern for his spiritual well being. She worried that his soul might get lost on the way to Heaven.

Sunday School offered the language of sincere fundamentalism as an antidote to my alternative magic language. It was a custom to sing many choruses. Among my favorite songs were *I'm Too Young To March In the King's Army*, *In the Sweet Bye and Bye*, *Jesus Loves Me*, *Jingle Bells*, and my favorite song, *Climb, Climb Up Sunshine Mountain*.

The second verse of *Jesus Loves Me* became a great source of solace as I fell asleep at night:

Red or yellow, black or white,
They are precious in his sight,
Jesus loves the little children of the world!

This song spoke to my spirit then as it does today, that Jews and Africans, French people, and Mormons are all God's beloved children. There is a sacred place where we all touch the pathos of living, and we learn to let go of prejudice and to embrace unity.

So it was that I entered a process of becoming saved, but deep inside, I held on to the conviction that I wanted to study Hebrew with the Jewish kids in our neighborhood. Sadly, I never learned Yiddish from walking around the block.

My attitude then and now has not changed—God likes to wink at us—and acknowledge that He's as involved and amused as we are with our growth lessons. Practicing new and unfamiliar languages contains a great spiritual reward for we learn also not to be afraid of what can separate us from being united and recognized as God's children. We can learn to practice speaking magical languages that are inclusive of each other in this world of strife and misunderstanding. I believe the language of inclusiveness is important and connects us in such a way as to be able to listen better to each other's differing opinions.

My parents insisted that our old discarded clothing could be shipped to the missionaries in the Belgian Congo rather than going to a kibbutz, which I would have preferred. *Why*, I asked myself, *would people in the hot plains of Africa want my old woolen winter clothes?*

It was in Israel where I wanted my outgrown clothes to go. Baptists were the "chosen" saved people who could package up their discarded possessions for the "Negroes" (the term used back then), but would not speak to them on the streetcar. We proudly recounted our salvation stories, but there was a paucity in our family for demonstrating love outside our own circle of friends.

While I learned the language of the independent Baptist church, I also worried about the concepts of either eternal damnation or gold-paved paths in Heaven for anyone not fortunate enough to recognize "the true way." *What if my grandfather went to Hell for smoking?* It frightened me to think that if there was only one true way to God, I might get on the wrong path. I worried about all the little children of the world, especially the ones in Africa who might not hear the truth or get a useless winter coat.

All this while, I had no doubts that my once blackened heart was being purified. Jesus loves me, I reminded myself at night when I said my Jewish prayers and said my goodnight to Jesus. Then I would lull myself to sleep by pondering the idea of infinity. *Even after the farthest stars, it still keeps going. Then after that, it goes some more. Where does space end and Heaven begin?*

Kindergarten was my first socialization experience. Politely, I waited patiently for my allotted time at the sand tray. Moving objects around in a sand tray is a therapeutic method of working on all relationships. Miss Clara Klutsch, our maiden lady teacher appeared to appreciate little Dutch-bobbed blond girls who spoke Yiddish during recess. Skipping rope by quickly interchanging the handles became my best sport. Dodge ball frightened me and I feared not being chosen for the best team. Jewish people had the reputation for being athletic and smart, I was informed by Freddy Schwartz. Polish people attracted me as well, and I wanted to kiss a Catholic, Kenny Stolarsky, who was in my class and lived in the Bennett Street apartments.

First grade curriculum introduced our class to reading out loud. For me, the characters from the *Dick and Jane* books became much more than imaginary friends. By November, my reading group had nearly finished all the primers when I was suddenly withdrawn from Caldwell Elementary School, located two short blocks from our house. I was ill without a diagnosis and my parents appeared worried. However, I did like all the attention I was receiving. My teacher came to visit. Mr. Schwartz drove us in his Buick to all sorts of doctors who stuck me with needles and took my temperature constantly. Leukemia had been suspected so everyone felt relieved with the diagnosis of glandular fever, an illness that still required hospitalization and several months of bed rest.

Two pleasant memories remain from that boring incarceration in my bedroom. Great Aunt Annie, Mother Gracie's sister—then in her late seventies, widowed, and childless—arrived with a crown of curly blue hair. I remember that she had an ample bosom.

On the front of her summer frock, she always wore a brooch and her bosom and wide lap were a source of comfort. Annie taught me how to make my bed with geometrically square hospital corners, to brush my hair one hundred strokes, and tie it with a pink ribbon. Together, we listened to *Buster Brown* on the radio, ate cinnamon toast dripping with a sugary, buttery glaze, and she laughed heartily. Annie made up stories about

Goldilocks and the Three Bears since my walls were papered with that design.

Secondly, the tonsil extraction marked a pivotal change in my independence. I was tricked into going into Wesley Memorial Hospital the day after Christmas. Once again, Mr. Schwartz donated time and transportation. My father discovered he could save money having both Bob's and my tonsils extracted by the same surgeon at the same time. My folks left with Mr. Schwartz, and we ate disgusting chop suey for dinner in the kid's ward of the hospital. I remember crying and feeling terrified. No one bothered to explain how painful this surgery could be to a small child.

Over the next four months, I read. Once home, the reading materials changed. *The Little Engine That Could* got placed back on the bookshelf and I became acquainted with *The Arabian Nights*. I read without ceasing. Collections of stories and collections of poems. *Black Beauty* and *The Little Prince*. I cried through *Little Women* and *Pandora's Box* shocked me with the harsh punishment of the characters. Until I got well enough to return to school, I read everything I could find on the bookshelves in my parents' home.

Second grade met in room 107 with Mrs. B.C. Bethards. The year revolved around spelling bees, and she lined us up into opposing teams against the blackboards under the cursive-writing guides and the framed picture of George Washington painted by Gilbert Stuart. There, we spent hours in fierce competition. Finally, I lost after hundreds of hours and several months of being top speller. Raymond Wertz, the chubby boy who sat next to me won by spelling correctly the word "sugar." Wouldn't you think after eating all that cinnamon toast with Aunt Annie that I would know enough to leave the letter "h" out of sugar? Heartbroken, my spelling grade for that quarter dropped from "Excellent Achievement" to only "Good Progress." For a while, I lost my focus on spelling bees and preferred time reading to myself. The spelling blow was my first big disappointment at Caldwell Elementary School.

At the conclusion of second grade, the class voted me onto the student council. Life was looking up and I wore a navy blazer and skinny pigtails. Inside of me, I was also convinced that I was the best speller. In fourth grade, Raymond Wertz believed Carolyn Cargile shot a spitball at him when a substitute was there. Wrong! I did this deed. Raymond, a great speller was also Jewish. And I developed a crush on him. By second grade, I wanted to kiss both a Catholic and a Jew.

For the next seven months, my mother was in bed with a difficult pregnancy. I learned to quarter a tomato with a sharp knife, prepare a cottage cheese filled salad on a tray with real lemon, and to make iced tea.

Mary Ellen, my new doll, could wet her diapers when given a bottle of water. Mary Ellen listened for hours to my magic language. Our new baby brother, David, was born on the Sabbath and weighed in at eleven pounds and ruined our Halloween by being born that night. He has thrown his weight around ever since his birth. While my mother turned her attention to this child she so desperately wanted after two miscarriages, I continued to mother my dolly, Mary Ellen, and became a confident caregiver.

31

II

THE LANGUAGE OF DISCOVERY: FIRST VACATION

THE IMAGE OF PUFFY cumulus clouds drifting over the Michigan sky floats through my mind. What a luxurious experience it is, in my early sixties, to revisit my childhood Mackinac Island story. Snapshots of these memories are glued inside my heart. Here is a mental place where I can turn to and flip over the worn pages of my internal life album. Life took on a slower pace then. What I am remembering is like an eight millimeter black and white home movie rolling back to the summer of 1950.

World War II had ended five years before, and now my family was doing well enough to buy our first automobile, a green second-hand Mercury, replete with white-rimmed tires. My brother, Bob, was forced to do a lot of chores, including the washing of the Mercury every Saturday.

"The car was too good of a deal to pass up," my father informed us. Owning the car created the opportunity for us to make the loop around Lake Michigan. Inside my eight-year-old mind, life felt agreeable with the freedom a car affords for everyone. My parents, my two brothers, and I were about to leave on our first real vacation.

"Dorothy, I have decided to pull a trailer behind the Mercury and we can choose state parks to stop at each night," my dad informed my mother. Making decisions in our family revolved around my father's agenda and his exclusive wishes. Neighbors were caravanning and pulling a Silverstream house trailer, while my Dad had hitched the twenty-foot "Blue Dot" behind our Mercury. Mother had insisted on having the trailer named after her. To this day, I still name all our cars.

I had butterflies in my stomach from my Dad's insistence on pulling out of our lane to pass every car on old autoroute U.S. 31, a two lane highway filled with pot holes caused by winter storms and now jammed with tourists. His sudden lane switching occurred seconds before an approaching angry truck driver flashed his bright lights and slammed on his loud horn. During those terrifying seconds, I pressed down hard on the imaginary brakes in the rear seat.

"Bob," I whined at my brother, "stay on your side." An imaginary line drawn down the center of the back seat kept us from fighting or hitting each other. Moments later Dad would swerve back into the lane, and I would relax my foot. After two days of erratic driving, we excitedly arrived near the Upper Peninsula to purchase ferry tickets.

A large white ferryboat departed once every hour from Arnold's dock in St. Ignace where Blue Dot was parked far from the water. Of course, we could have parked much closer, but my father did not want to pay for parking. No cars were permitted on the island. Crossing the straits to Mackinac Island took about forty-five minutes. Looking overhead, we observed sea gulls on that balmy sunny day, and soon we passed the red light house and the captain maneuvered the boat past the fuel dock to the pier. Between Arnold's dock and Main Street was the tantalizing aroma of fudge shops.

"Can we buy some candy, please?" my brother and I asked. Each one-half pound creamy fudge wedge came wrapped in shiny white paper with a small plastic knife. Our group became the newest boatload of *fudgees,* the name the islanders gave to summer tourists. Our fingers were sticky from licking off the remnants of cotton candy, fudge, and chocolate ice cream. About that time, my ten-month-old brother, David, became very fussy. The world revolved around him, it seemed to me, because he was born after my mother sustained two miscarriages. This was the child who brought her the greatest pleasure. People always stopped us to admire his golden curly hair.

Part of the excitement was the prohibition of cars on the island. Dad bargained hard to find the best deal on a horse drawn carriage tour.

"I will offer you a dollar apiece and half-price for the children except the baby, whom I will hold," Dad challenged each tram driver. Frequently, my father's business transactions caused people to look at us in peculiar ways. Once seated, we bumped together since it was cheaper to take the flatbed ride than the carriage with the surrey. I noticed dozens of bike rental shops and wondered why we didn't cycle. Then I remembered that my dad perspired and his shirt became smelly.

Lots of local kids played with sling shots sold in the Trading Post advertised as "genuine, Indian-made." Horses heaved us up Turkey Hill and then pulled us gently through silent woodland trails of elm trees rich with melodious bird song, apple, cherry, and plum orchards, and butterflies flitting from bush to bush in vivid Lifesavers-candy colors. Wildflowers cascaded in masses over white picket fences and bicyclists tinkled their bells passing our carriage. We toured Fort Mackinac, climbed to Arch Rock, and rode past elaborate cottages on the bluffs built by distinguished lumberjack families in the late 1860's. Becoming accustomed to the horse odor was unpleasant on that hot and humid summer afternoon. The steady clip clop of the horses also made me drowsy. Eventually, we paused in front of the Grand Hotel.

"You remember, Walter, I stayed here with my parents when my dad played golf," Mother rubbed-in their supposed elegance. It would have been possible to walk through the lobby to gaze upon fancy people sipping afternoon tea. After all, the hotel boasted the longest porch in the world. Dad did not want to tip the driver the additional fifty-cent charge so we just clip-clopped past lush gardens to admire the guests in their funny-looking golf clothes and continued down the hill past the brown chapel and back into town past the blacksmith shop. The quaint charm can be seen beautifully captured in the movie, *Somewhere In Time*, which was filmed on the island.

I remember this day in my childhood with great accuracy. Other summers we have taken our own children, biked the island, and spent the night at a historic inn. I repeated the adventure the past two years. My dear friend, Jan, accompanied me and we stayed in one of the historic cottages, now owned by a neighbor. We would rock on the front porch and watch the carriages go by on those lazy summer days.

Mackinac Island is a retreat place where I go to reflect on life and reorient myself. It is a holy place to which I go to discover healing and remember the joy and happiness of yesteryears. It helps me somehow to redirect my self-absorption to thinking of the welfare and happiness of others. Each visit there reminds me that there still exists freshness and vitality in life and a warm summer breeze all too pungent with the smell of horse-drawn carriages. The dismal winter season of my spirit wearies me, but the Island always beckons as a place of strength and encouragement.

III

THE LANGUAGE OF SURRENDER:
LATE CHILDHOOD

JESUS AND I BEGAN talking daily. I felt like I belonged to God in a way that I did not belong in my family. There seemed to always be tangible evidence that God was with me in a personal sense. Often, I thought about children living in poor areas.

What would it be like not to have a Mary Ellen doll who knew your deepest secrets? I asked myself. As a small child, I yearned to shine for Jesus and help people less fortunate. Already, I knew about suffering and dying in the world. Compassion was a seedling beginning to form in my soul.

Eventually, I slowly came to accept that I would never be a Jewish girl, so I stopped pretending to be Jewish. For the next three years, I became a student of the various languages of the Bible. In Sunday school, we learned a new chorus. My brother, Bob, had a high-pitched soprano voice and I was almost as tall as him.

The B-I-B-L-E,
Yes, that's the book for me!

I stand alone on the word of God,
The B-I-B-L-EEEEE….

During those early formative years, I was already looking to the Bible as an instructional guide and trusted it with all my heart. Jesus even said, "Let the little children come to me, and do not hinder them, for the kingdom of heaven belongs to such as these." My child-like faith invariably trusted God to lead me.

With a flashlight hidden under my pillow late at night, I memorized long passages, especially *The Psalms*. People became malicious and angry and rebellious in these scripture stories before they lamented their transgressions and offered their prayers for deliverance. So with all the firmness of my will and a courageous heart, I memorized chapter after chapter to win the much-coveted scholarship to church summer camp at Lake Ripley in Wisconsin. Those words that I hid in my heart have given me a wealth of strength over all these decades. The Scripture has shown me a path and a way when I became lost in my own desert or became self-sufficient and wanted to rebel against my God. In reading and memorizing scripture, I have found the deepest longings of my heart met, and I have discovered security in calling to mind the words I learned decades before. Some of the words are so precious to me that I believe their meaning has preserved my life.

My older brother, Bob, in a surreptitious way memorized one more chapter than me after I fell asleep one night. To add further insult to my injured feelings, he memorized a chapter from a book in the Old Testament, which was more difficult to commit to memory. Complicated genealogies and bloody sacrifices were part of the stories. Since we were the top two competitors, he broke the tie and went to camp that summer. What a pity since Bob had not yet decided to become a missionary in

Africa. My heart was already committed to be in some distant land. He used the Word of God to get even with his sister. Such cruelty, I thought. I stayed at home and helped potty-train our younger brother, David. To accomplish this feat, I lashed him to the potty and offered him some *Little Golden* books and some animal crackers.

On my eleventh birthday, we moved twenty miles west to the suburb of Western Springs. Our father designed the rambling reddish ranch house accentuated with a flagstone fireplace and a large picture window. No one was consulted with on the color palette—the roof was pinkish, and the garage was painted in beige and brown squares. Dad was proud to have designed this house and to leave the city of Chicago to become a suburbanite.

Bob had just been promoted from eighth grade. With mixed emotions, I left behind my Jewish heritage in Chicago to enter a community where everyone looked and voted the same. It took me another forty years to correct that mistake and seek out the irregular person. The world is unpredictable, and matching sweater outfits do not correct our basic insecurities. To my dismay, no one in the village of Western Springs was Jewish or Black.

A new brother, Scott, was born into the family. He was adorable and I liked babysitting him and sometimes pretended to be his mother. Every bedroom was now filled and my mother seemed happier with her life.

Bob and I were given no choice in the matter of class grade at school. Once again, we were double promoted. Of course, I did not want a soul to discover that I was so young for my seventh grade junior high class at McClure Junior High School. Only barely eleven years old, I had not started my menstrual cycle. Up to age eleven, I followed most of the rules imposed by my father. I certainly avoided getting into any trouble with him because of his fierce temper. Corporal punishment was the practice my father used to control our behavior. I feared the smack of a hairbrush or belt on my bare bottom. Now, I realize that he grew up in a family that whipped children for misbehavior. But to me, punishments never seemed to fit the severity of the crime. I didn't think anyone should ever be spanked or yelled at regardless of their behavior. Hitting children only destroys their self-esteem. To rebel, I became sassy. In addition, I loved being sent to my room to discover another book that I could read in silence. Books were an escape from some of the solitariness I felt at home.

I viewed myself as a privileged, but lonely girl, in a dainty, pink bedroom. Pale pink Venetian blinds covered the corner windows. Coverlets made from sheer pink ruffled fabric adorned the twin beds. My new maple desk had a drop-lid writing surface. On top of that chest was a case with glass doors showing off my collection of exquisitely dressed storybook dolls. My doll and life confidante, Mary Ellen, sat quietly on my pillow.

Up until that eleventh birthday, I think I followed all the family's rules and expectations. That afternoon, two neighbor girls strolled through the peony and lilac hedges to meet me. Debbie was a blond with the saddle shoes, and Dana wore a dark, pixie hairstyle.

"Debbie, would you like to play with my dolls?"

"No, but we're inviting some boys over to Dana's later and you can come," she replied confidently. Giggling, they told me some games were planned. June 13th, 1953 marks my last intentional monologue in Yiddish and the first time I truly snubbed Mary Ellen.

That summer, I discovered Seventeen magazine, razor blades, bras, falsies, white buck shoes, cherry Cokes, stealing a scarf from the local five and ten, and yes, the unbridled language of adolescence. Entering a new world was both disturbing and exhilarating. This was the time when I began to express that there were tempests and unhappiness brewing within.

IV

The Language of Adolescence: Junior High and High School

BEGINNING SEVENTH GRADE at McClure Junior High School was most exciting. I rode my blue Schwinn bicycle one-and-a-half miles to the traditional two-story brick building, then, carefully locked-up my bike with my new combination lock.

I carefully observed what suburban girls wore to school. If you were female, that meant adopting the current style, which was almost a uniform. My new friends and I wore plaid pleated skirts, white Peter Pan blouses, and cardigans made of lambs' wool. Girls wore their hair in ponytails tied with brightly colored chiffon scarves. Three shoe styles were acceptable in the fashionable crowd: white bucks with red soles, penny loafers, and saddle shoes. I carried a white buck powder bag in my pencil bag, so my shoes were clean even when the snow was mushy and gray. Plastic bracelets were becoming popular. Seventh grade was also the year to purchase your first bra. The sales clerk at the local department store helped a girl select the correct cup size. That became a part of your generally known personal information.

No one had ever given me any jewelry, other than the small gold cross on the occasion of my Baptism by immersion over which Dr. I.C. Peterson presided when I was eight. Beginning at age eight, every Baptist child received, after a year of perfect attendance, a circular white enamel pin at a special ceremony. On the pin, a blue banner overarches a red cross on which is superimposed a gold crown, symbolizing the crown of life given in Heaven to those who faithfully stay the course. I have envisioned myself, hundreds of times, waiting patiently in line to be crowned. You may snicker at this bold naivety, but I have pursued a spiritual journey for sixty years. Perseverance, I believe, is both a discipline and a virtue.

Subsequent years of perfect attendance meant receiving a brightly enameled bar. My pin represents immeasurable sentimental value, although as I turn it over in my hand, I can scarcely make out the words "Cross and Crown" by Uncas due to green mold on the underside. Maybe the pin was fabricated from a cheap metal. Both my convictions about a practical theology needing to be broader and the mold on the pin have increased with life experience.

Faithful attendance is a sacred obligation for any evangelical or fundamentalist connected to the Baptist religious persuasion. Attendance is defined as both presence and active participation in worship, mid-week prayer meetings, youth group, summer camp, and Sunday night service. If you had any musical talent, you were expected to either sing in a choir or play the piano. I sang and my brother took up the offering at Sunday School Junior Church, the microcosm community of what our parents did in the upstairs sanctuary. Bob and I also tithed our allowance, which meant giving back to the church 10 percent of what we either earned from chores or received as gifts at Christmas. I still believe it is wicked to force a child to tithe on a gift.

From my knowledge in speaking to other Sunday school pin accumulators, Baptists seem to represent the population of the recipients and guardians of these attendance pins. Only recently, have I found my hard-earned pin—stashed away in my top dresser drawer next to my high school Josten ring. They do look a little tacky worn with pearls or diamonds.

Bars ceased appearing after eight years. Pressure to attend Sunday school every week must have lessened. Nevertheless, my pin reminded me during those turbulent teenage years that I had become saved for some eternal purpose. My personal theology has broadened to be much more inclusive of other faith communities. But the attendance pin still reminds me of the cost as well as the fruitfulness of perseverance in the quest for God in one's personal life. Perhaps I may surprise myself and wear my pin one day. Deep inside, those childhood convictions are anchors that have been satisfactory guides in rocky times.

Learning the language of trying to fit into a social group in which I would feel popular or at least tolerated became a challenge for me socially in junior high and senior high school. All of us need so desperately to find that safe place where we feel we belong. Having my own bedroom satisfied the need for some adolescent privacy. Learning how to be popular was not a topic we discussed at home. Chores were the recurring theme of conversation. My parents appeared preoccupied with their own distinctive problems in life. My older brother, Bob, was already popular and usually avoided me. *Seventeen* magazine was the only self-help advice column I read. Clearly, I needed more attention at home.

Several times each year, Walter, my dad, and Dorothy, my mother, hauled us four children in the green Mercury to visit my grandparents at Fox Lake. My grandmother, whom we had been instructed to address Mother Gracie, preferred my older brother, Bob. Up at the lake, we were treated to huge, cooked feasts and rich desserts, which appeared effortlessly as Floating Island meringues, poppy seed cake, rhubarb pie, and chocolate frosted brownies. Golden nut cups held M&M's. Mother Gracie doted on Bob, I believe, because her own son, Bob, had died at age nineteen from Lupus Nephritis, a kidney disease. My beautiful grandmother, who had displayed so much vigor in life suffered from a mother's broken heart. Although her home was warm and festive, she still felt the pain, grieving for her dead son. Her grief was so bound up with her love and pride in this son. Bereaved parents have lacerated hearts. Losing a child is the most devastating of life's losses.

One hot summer night, driving home, I was squeezed in the rear seat between two of my brothers, Bob and David. I always got the middle hump of the rear seat, and we made up imaginary lines to protect our personal space. "Why?" I ask myself, "am I so afraid to catch their cooties?" In 1955, our car was without air conditioning. On every trip, one brother soiled a diaper, another got carsick, while another emitted some disgusting, foul odor. Dad refused to wear deodorant and sweated profusely. To protect my sensitive nose, I rolled down the window.

"Just what do you think you are doing?" my father yelled at me.

"I'm watching the moon," I replied.

Driving home from Mother Gracie's that summer night, I distracted myself by watching a full moon skim along the darkening horizon just near the Big Dipper. That full moon followed us all the way home to the new red brick ranch house with the pink roof. I remember wondering if that moon would follow me wherever I went and called home. Our first-born arrived the year a man walked on the surface of the moon. The moon reminds me of the holy time when wise men were guided by that light from beyond.

Counting silently on all ten fingers, I concluded that because I was already one year advanced in school, I would only have to endure twenty-seven more months of high school life at Lyons Township High School. Freedom lay ahead and I began to fantasize a trip to California. Dad never allowed us to touch the thermostat to control the heat in our home and I was perpetually cold. Wind chill factor had become a new scientific buzzword in Chicago. In my mind, I envisioned myself lounging around a shimmering swimming pool or playing volleyball on a sandy beach. "Look at that tall blond," I imagined people noticing me.

Few members of my family inquired what I personally thought about anything. My opinions were certainly not highly valued at home. Soon, I turned to the high school youth leaders at the Village Baptist Church to become my mentors. Becoming truly popular was fading into a hazy ruefulness.

When I was dropped from the top clique in the eighth grade, my life felt reduced to bankruptcy. Two principle factors contributed to my early social demise, I reasoned. Miss Bernadette Gift, maiden lady and history teacher, accused me, Grace Marilyn Shaw, president of the eighth grade, of cheating and stealing some answers from Mary Helen Meadowcroft's test paper.

"Bring me that test paper immediately!" she yelled out as she ripped up the pages and tossed my exam into the waste paper basket. I had never felt so much mortification or shame. This was clearly a false accusation because I never cheated until tenth grade Plane Geometry class.

Secondly, related to the social failure, after some boys crashed my eighth grade graduation slumber party at 3:00 AM, my mother rushed angrily back to the screened-in porch to shut up the girls from giggling.

"You girls are just asking for trouble," she yelled at us. "I am going to call every one of your mothers and describe your hussy behavior." During the following, mortifying moments, the boys were sent scrambling from the porch. My mother's rudeness felt like a deathblow and provided sufficient cause for my popularity to be seriously compromised. Now that the coolest girls were out of the picture, I did not have the help to master the art of shaving my legs or armpits without enduring a bloody mess. "Who would be my friends?" I worried.

Two or three times a week in high school, another group of halfway-popular friends saved me a place at the cafeteria lunch table. The Christian group was usually off in some classroom having a Bible study. But on the days my mother preferred I buy my lunch—usually because she had run out of bologna—I spent so much of the precious twenty-five minutes waiting in the cafeteria line that my reserved place was usually occupied when I arrived. On those days, feeling undesirable, I usually put on my pea coat and went outdoors to smoke a cigarette. My first cigarette was smoked in front of the bathroom mirror attempting to blow smoke rings and appear sultry. To be candid, some of the lunch hours were spent in the girls' bathroom using concealing cosmetics to cover the pimples marring my cheeks. Having some acne problems certainly didn't improve my self-confidence.

My mother seemed oblivious to my complexion problems. One Christmas, she tried to help raise my popularity scale by hosting a holiday tea with me. I am grateful since this effort improved my social index ever so slightly. Girls in the cool group rotated homes, hosting potlucks before basketball games. A couple times, when invited, I even brought Freda Schwartz's tuna fish casserole with the peas and topped with potato chips as my offering to the current goddess of popularity.

Rick Hensel walked me home from school occasionally. To alter the fact that he was two inches shorter, he walked on the curb, while I sloshed through the gray snow in the street. Rick and I attended the same church, and his father was Sunday school superintendent. Sometimes, when I babysat on Friday nights, for thirty-five cents an hour, Rick would show up about $1.10 into the evening and after the children were bedded down, we would practice French kissing. I loved Rick for years until he impregnated a girl at a Christian college and married her.

The summer of 1957, I emptied my entire account of $85.00 in babysitting revenues and bought a train ticket to vacation in California. Dr. Peterson and his family entertained me. Arriving at the train station in Los Angeles, the Palm trees reminded me of Sunday school stories depicting Palm trees on flannel boards. Outside the station were indigo trees called Jacarandas. Mornings were cool. Disneyland had recently opened and provided pure fantasy. Roy Rogers and Dale Evans were active members of the pastor's church. Ginger Roger's TV double accompanied me to the Farmers Market on Third Street. Billy Graham Senior, founder of my church in Illinois, held a huge rally in Anaheim that was broadcast on television. Through his preaching, I once again was reassured of my eternal salvation. How impressive Southern California appeared. I was happy, and life became different after that vacation. Two weeks later, I tried to convince my parents to move to California. My father replied to my request as usual.

"You don't know what you are even talking about. Why would we ever leave Illinois?" It saddens me to think that my own father saw me as not having a voice in our family, and he repeated that harsh judgment for decades whenever he disagreed with me. I learned to avoid men that refused to take my opinions seriously.

There were still many concerns in high school to overcome. I was still reading my Bible every day, trying to keep my white buck shoes as clean as my reputation and worried that I didn't own enough full-fashioned cashmere sweaters with matching skirts to be included in the cool dress code. The majority of the Baptists at the Village Baptist Church did not dance or smoke or drink. Not much experimentation happened. Whether or not this is accurate recollection, I think I attended two homecoming dances, two proms, the girl-ask-boy affairs, and a Valentine's Day dance. Paul Bock invited me to the senior prom before Rick Hensel initiated a request to accompany me. Mother insisted that protocol dictates the good manners of accepting one's first offer. What a disaster to spend your senior prom and the whole next day at the beach with life's second best for you.

Senior year was academically challenging, and I enjoyed participating in class discussions. Every male history or literature instructor attracted me. Less intimidated, I spoke with animation in my voice. Three years of dreadful math were completed. Plane Geometry and Algebra nearly sent me into a cheating mode, which would have permanently tainted my personal moral code of respectable behavior.

Now that Rick was off to college, there was no more French kissing, and I began to appreciate studying the French language with Miss Francoise Lutz. She had a reputation for being a demanding teacher. All those years of habitual Bible memorization really helped me memorize vocabulary and learn to conjugate irregular verbs. Our textbook remains on my bookshelves and is entitled *Points de Vue*. *La Troisième Section* was entitled *Amour*. This language spoke to my soul. The first poem I memorized is short and called "Pensée" which translates "Thought:"

Et si je t'aimais,

*Si tu m'aimais
comme 'je t'aimerais!*

*If I were to love you,
and if you were to love me,
how I would love you!*

I did love the French language. Although my mother professed to speak fluent French, whenever she attempted to speak it, the result felt forced. By the second year, I haltingly strung together a few phrases somewhat awkwardly. Discovering the French language brought me immeasurable pleasure.

An extra-curricular activity in which I became slightly involved was the Girls Athletic Association. Any female who played archery was spared the humiliation of taking a gang shower. To be appropriately acceptable in the school yearbook, I pursued drama activities, sang in the high school and church choir, and served as an officer in the French club and Future Teachers Association. I threw away my yearbook many decades ago, but there was a long enough list of activities under my senior photo in the annual to feel worthy of some esteem.

Paul Bock continued to pursue me with some enthusiasm. The pale blue strapless organza dress stayed held against my body pretty well with scotch tape the night of the prom. For a few hours, I felt smashing in my dyed-blue satin shoes, a rose wrist corsage, and an inspired French twist coiffeur executed by the beauty parlor in town.

I don't remember much about graduation from high school except being embarrassed that my mother had sewn my dress and it was too fussy for my taste. Mother insisted that *Vogue* dressmaking patterns were superior to *McCalls*. Officially on the college academic track all through high school, I remember one elective course

53

called *Clothing 1*. What a dreadful experience I had with my first sewing project. The blouse pattern included a complicated collar, gussets under the armholes, and French cuffs. One day I sewed over my wrist with the sewing machine needle, which left a permanent scar. Maybe, I wore the completed project twice. Sewing class was a nightmare.

Where were the academic advisors in 1959? No SAT exams were administered at Lyons Township. Somehow my ACT scores along with two faculty recommendations were sent to North Central College, a small liberal arts college about fifteen miles west in Naperville, Illinois.

In the 1950's, Naperville was the center of manufacturing for Kroehler furniture, a well-known design company. My father suggested the junior college located on the high school campus.

He said, "This would save us a lot of money if you attend junior college until you decide on a career and think about how you are going to support yourself." I would have been mortified to continue living at home. One week before my seventeenth birthday, I graduated. What stands out for me, as the finest diploma equivalent, was the graduation gift from my folks—a matched set of white American Tourister luggage.

That summer, after my senior year, I put the study of French aside and worked as an aide in a tuberculosis sanitarium where I developed mononucleosis. One summer before, I modeled in a department store and I eagerly sought advice from a young couple in medical school that I hoped could help me discern if I wanted to be a missionary nurse in Africa or possibly attempt to become a model. There were simply no other options in my head. Flight attendants could not be afraid to fly in airplanes and secretaries needed to be able to type. My older brother was transferring to Stanford on a full scholarship. Who would assist me in figuring out my life?

V

THE LANGUAGE OF GROWING UP:
COLLEGE MEMORIES

DECADES HAVE PASSED by since my college years. Whenever I consciously revisit that time frame in my mind's eye, I see myself walking through the dusty corridors at Wheaton College. I am pleased to recall the friendships and the learning during that brief interlude between adolescence and adulthood. Seldom do I allow myself to reflect on my immaturity during the freshman year at North Central College.

Mother dropped me off at Kroehler Hall and helped me drag the three new pieces of white American Tourister luggage to my assigned dorm room along with a chenille bed spread, new sheets, blanket and pillow, plus an assortment of stuffed animals. Mary Ellen, my doll, embarrassed me by age seventeen, so I decided she would be happier and safer at home. I found myself waiting in the dorm room to meet my roommate. I was looking for the courage and boldness to ask my mother to leave. Mother had not usually walked beside me in a way that was comforting or reassuring in times of discomfort.

Pat walked in. Anyone would confirm that she was one step beyond homely in appearance, was overweight, and wore owl glasses. In addition to being ugly and bossy, she wore a permed hairstyle. *This is whom I waited all summer to meet?* I thought. No other girls were gathering in our room. Here, I had been waiting for a bold and fun roommate, and this had the forebodings of being a mundane, unremarkable experience. I needed a friend to walk with me and here was Pat. What a disappointment!

Pat freaked about how our dorm room ought to look. Textbooks in neat piles, closed notebooks, and sharpened pencils were all organized on her side of the desk. She became upset whenever the hall monitor left a sloppy warning notice on our door. Football practices had begun, and I was far more interested in watching the team practice and chatting with the players than I was in cleaning our room, or for that matter, spending any time with Pat.

Every single evening, Pat soaked her underwear and socks in the small sink in our room under the one tiny mirror I used to apply makeup. Pat discovered some perverse pleasure in puttering around our room and infrequently left. She wallowed in cleanliness.

Then it happened. Shame, regret, and guilt are part of reliving "The Incident." I should have tried to live more peacefully with someone I disliked.

One night after entering our room, something extremely violent erupted inside me. Coming home after a date, I wanted to brush my teeth before getting ready for bed. Rage was what I felt seeing her soapy underwear soaking in the sink. When Pat insistently refused to remove them, she said, "Go brush your teeth down the hall. I'm busy."

The only defense I offer for this bad behavior is that my own nose had been bent out of shape since the first day in the common bathroom. Her challenge released the cap on my temper. Here is my shocking revelation: I reached out and without warning slapped her in the face.

"Get your crap out of the sink!" I yelled at her. This sudden, shocking blow landed on her nose. Blood poured out all over her new rug. Blood mingled with her soaking panties. Within moments, the dorm was buzzing and the dean of women appeared. My wicked behavior landed me in a single dorm room for the remainder of the first semester. At some point under threat of being expelled, I mumbled some apology that I did not sincerely mean. Pat avoided any future contact. Maybe, if had I known that I'd get my own room, I'd have punched her sooner.

I had both witnessed my brothers and myself hitting and being slugged at home. Anger management was never a priority in our family's conversations.

Second semester, Ann, a sweet gal from Michigan came to live with me. Recently, she had placed second in the National Cherry Pie baking competition. Ann volunteered to be my roommate. I discovered her to be easy as pie, and our friendship developed and deepened over many years. Ann's greatest flaw was leaving the lamp turned on after "lights out."

Academics were not overly challenging at North Central. It was fun for the first time to peruse the course catalog and decide what courses I wanted to pursue. "Finish what you start," was my father's wise advice. This determination worked well in the study of French language and literature, English literature, and World history. There was great value singing in the soprano section of the college touring choir. But one course completely stumped me. I don't know why, but I signed up for Zoology class. The description of the course guaranteed that the class would fulfill my science requirement. I was overwhelmed on the first day of lab. Zoology labs reek of strange odors. Dead frogs and dead pigs stink. Lectures were somewhat interesting and held in

59

a big hall. Actual experiments with the animals took place every Saturday morning at 8:00 AM. Early morning lab times interrupted my sleep after late Friday night social activities. Your lab partner was assigned to you. Why, I thought, would anyone want to get up for this disgusting activity?

Obviously, I had not expended sufficient time on this class. When the alarm rang, I rolled over in bed. Cutting 80 percent of the lab requirement earned me a D grade that first semester. I had not yet realized how important it was to not give up, and that terrible grade remains on my college transcript. How I wished someone had steered me into Botany sooner. Botany students learn the classification of plants and flowers. Botany lab was an easy commitment. Field excursions often took us the arboretum. Botany was an honorable alternative to Zoology, although the cuter boys remained in Zoology. It may be that they already understood their calling as pre-med students. Geeks were more attracted to studying plants. Years later, I find pleasure in discovering new plants that find a home in my garden. Gardening became my favorite hobby.

Pride was at stake for me after the Zoology fiasco, and I set the goal of developing consistent and faithful study habits. For the first time I began to understand how art and literature and music are interrelated. I felt excited to be a student and felt confident that if I were to attend classes faithfully and study three or four hours a day, that my efforts would prove fruitful.

North Central College was filled with caring and competent faculty. I did well there. My best memory of freshman year was a date with a young man who attended Wheaton College, which was situated about eight miles north. Wheaton College is a top tier school in academic success and an arch competitor of North Central College. I remember having a spectacular time walking in the dewy grass with this boy, but I do not recall whether we had a second date. My life was not organized around dating yet.

Everything about Wheaton attracted me when I visited the campus. Here was a beautiful campus on a hill with enormous Elm trees (my Botany class was already paying off) shading the hundred-year-old buildings. The student union building housed alternatives to eating in a cafeteria. New to the campus was an elegantly designed brick concert hall and chapel. The bookstore alone captivated my enthusiasm. I spent hours roaming the shelves.

"What am I going to do with my life?" was still a question I pondered often. I consulted with my high school mentors from my church, Fran and Doug. They had been such steady role models and encouraged me to consider transferring mid-way through my sophomore year. This seemed to be a choice that I could not resist and in fact, the experience radically altered my life. Finally, I would have the same academic status as my brother Bob away at Stanford University.

Elated to be headed to a prestigious Christian institution, I did not anticipate any difficult adjustments. One serious irritation involved "The Pledge." Wheaton College's pledge concerned a code of behavior to which every student was expected to subscribe both in private and public places. Many evangelical schools insist on a similar code. I believe in not cheating, so I could have conformed easily to that standard. The pledge seemed ridiculous to me. No student or faculty member was allowed to drink, smoke, dance, or attend movies or theatre. To this day, I do not understand justification for controlling the behavior in such a severe manner. In signing the pledge, I meant to adhere to the rules. Slip-ups occurred. That caused me to feel ashamed. When I felt too overly monitored, I rebelled. My personal interpretation of the rules meant that I would observe them faithfully while I was on campus. Off campus, I set my own parameters on my personal behavior.

In addition to the pledge, every student and faculty member also subscribed to a core statement of theological beliefs. The Nicene Creed formed the basis for the creed of the Trinity. God was viewed as Heavenly father, creator and sustainer of the world. Jesus, begotten Son of God, was born fully human and fully divine and came to Earth to reconcile the world to God. Humankind is given the indwelling presence of the Holy Spirit as guide and peace. Ideas about God have filled my mind since age four, so I particularly enjoyed the theology classes.

But the fact that there were no Jews on campus disturbed me. After all, this was a Christian college, and Jesus was Jewish. Some classmates were Black. Any observer would have commented on the lack of ethnic diversity as well as the geographical diversity of the student population, especially those in graduate school.

Acceptance as a transfer student to Wheaton College was another pivotal marker in my personal development. For me, it marked a dramatic change in my self-esteem and confidence. I so desired to be a good Christian and at Wheaton, I truly felt like I belonged to a group of kind people who wanted to make a significant difference in the world.

My roommate was also named Grace. Grace Fulrath had no time or interest in laundering lingerie in our room. Our friendship continues forty-five years later. She would agree that there has never been an argument between us and we always endeavor to see the perspective of the other and try to help each other. Grace established herself as a serious philosophy student, often reading the works of Kierkegaard until 3:00 AM. Her upbeat personality kept her laughing constantly. Her loyalty to me allowed her to find time to go outside in the freezing night to keep me company while I sneaked off campus to light up my daily, forbidden cigarette.

Both of us were committed to our academic lives in a wholehearted manner. These years held treasured, adventurous times together. Often, Grace shared the stash of caviar that she kept in her top dresser drawer. An open tin of caviar causes a peculiar odor, but we always forgave each other for our eccentricities. Grace lent me her fashionable clothes and her raccoon fur coat. Her mother had died from cancer when Grace was ten years old. Our conversations ceased only when one of us fell asleep.

Among her wacky ideas were her fad diet regimes and on occasion, I supported her through a diet. One favorite was the ice cream diet, which lasted for a solid week. We were permitted nine scoops of vanilla ice cream, topped with artificial flavorings each day. I remember preferring rum extract as my flavoring.

Grace had grown up in an apartment on Fifth Avenue in New York. Invitations to come to our suburban home for the weekend were fun for her. One weekend during our senior year, I brought Grace to our home in Western Springs. By some magical coincidence, my parents and brothers were out of town. While mixing up a batch of chocolate chip cookie dough, we were searching for vanilla extract and discovered a bottle in the cupboard called *Southern Comfort*. That was our first shared alcoholic beverage and because of "The Pledge," we decided to keep a secret: we each drank a full tumbler of whiskey as we ate the cookie dough. I accept responsibility for this incident, as I was the hostess. Hours later, we awoke with stomach aches and the determination not to ever repeat this behavior. Our first cocktail in our senior year became the last until my wedding night.

Choosing what major to pursue in college required some careful planning. "Think about what you are going to do to support yourself," my father advised me. Serious reflection about the future in my mind had not developed beyond purchasing a one-way airplane ticket to California. I did not choose to become a secretary or a nurse, which were popular options. Very few women wanted to exit Wheaton College without an engagement ring on their finger. Girls at Wheaton may not have smoked or danced, but many had some knowledge of kissing and making out with boys.

I loved the idea of speaking languages other than English but was also pursuing a second major in Literature. Initially in undergrad classes, I hesitated practicing pronunciation in my French classes. Gradually, I became aware of an almost musical intonation flowing over my tongue. Participating in conversation class eventually became an exhilarating experiment. There I was, in the second row, in Old Main Tower, raising my hand and volunteering for "Les Exercices Oraux" in front of my classmates. Self-conscientiousness had disappeared. Could it be that I was pretending? *No*, I rebuked myself, *I am making myself understandable.* Unlike the curious fraud, I felt practicing the magical language, this was real. For months I practiced daily, speaking out loud, talking to the mirror. Eventually, there were no more French classes from which to choose at Wheaton.

To ensure my confidence as a foreign language speaker, I applied to a summer French study program at McGill University in Montreal, Canada. Again, perseverance paid off and I was accepted. This summer experience sharpened my focus on mastery of the French language. It's amusing to remember decades later, but at that time, I wish someone had given me the following advice:

*—Be informed and stay committed to
what you are practicing into perfection.*

—Never try to pack starched crinoline petticoats to take in luggage on a study abroad program.

—Voulez-vous faire du camping?" is not so much about camping when it comes from a wide-eyed, 19 year-old Canadian boy.

Working hard on the language paid off several months later. High schools in Southern California were interviewing for secondary language teachers at Wheaton College. Grace dared me to attend an interview by bribing me with $5.00. I had not really considered teaching as a career. In fact, I had never even thought of taking a course in education. Ten days later, West Covina Unified School District offered me a teaching position by telephone.

It is fair to state that I occasionally mismanaged my relationships with boys. Having a steady boy friend helped me feel more secure and all those other girls in our local sorority were becoming engaged. Nils is a good man and very clear on his Campus Crusade understanding of theology. Nils desired to take Campus Crusade to the universities in the Philippines as soon as he finished his master's degree and raised financial support. Well, I did not want to miss out on those California boys. I liked kissing Nils but his parents insulted me by calling me too worldly and not suitable to be a preacher's wife. When the night arrived for Nils to ask my father's permission for my hand in marriage, my father flatly refused. "She can never live comfortably on your salary," he informed Nils.

Elvon used more wisdom in cultivating a relationship with my parents and was a frequent visitor both at Wheaton College as well as on vacations in Western Springs. I could tell that Elvon was an ardent suitor and pursued me with dates to the symphony, dinners out, and invitations to attend fun and cultural events. We were expecting to attend the George Washington Banquet, which was a substitute for a formal dance at Wheaton. During the afternoon of the event, Elvon delivered my wrist corsage. After forty-two years, I still feel terrible regret about how I mistreated him.

"Elvon," I said, "I just am not attracted to you and don't want to go out with you anymore. Sorry. Bye."

This was an ugly encounter. I never apologized to him. He was a decent young man who on two successive Christmases brought me two packages. I could tell that one contained an engagement ring and one contained something less permanent. I would return the ring boxes, but open the others. I have gold leaf earrings resting in the same drawer as my Sunday school pin.

Wheaton College days were coming to an end. I had invested myself wisely, while there and was encouraged by some of the quantifiable goals achieved. On that graduation morning, I felt competent to speak both the language of French and was beginning to understand more about the language of friendship.

When my name was called to receive my diploma, I quickly opened the navy and orange cover only to notice that a library fine had not been paid and that my degree was being securely held in the Registrar's Office.

VI
THE LANGUAGE OF INDEPENDENCE:
FRENCH LESSONS

THE LARGEST SUITCASE in the high school *American Tourister* luggage collection accompanied me to Paris stuffed with practically all my worldly possessions which included a travel journal, a box of laxatives, eight rolls of film and all the clothes I had bought in college with my babysitting money. By June 1963, I had arrived at an emotional place where I could leave behind the crinoline petticoats in Western Springs with everything else from childhood including my parents, my pink princess telephone, and Mary Ellen.

Our Pan Am flight would be leaving from Philadelphia International Airport, crossing the Atlantic Ocean, flying over Greenland, Ireland, Great Britain, and arriving in the late morning in Paris. I thought the whole world could see my heart beating with nervous excitement. People in Paris were actually speaking French.

There we stood, Vicki Buxman and me, in front of one of the most beautiful squares in the world. There was a broad tree-lined avenue called the Champs Elysees, which we traversed to reach our destination, the rented headquarters for the Billy Graham Crusade. Billy would be conducting his first crusade in Europe. Underneath our fourth floor office building was a candy shop where baskets of "bon bons" made us salivate each workday. The candy added an additional ten pounds to my weight. *Café au chocolat* went down smoothly with the candy.

Vicki, an adorable junior at Wheaton College had discovered the job possibility. The job description was to translate *Decision* magazine into the French language before Billy arrived for his European conference late in the summer. Mailing out the magazine was intended to stimulate interest in the crusade. Although the job description was intended for one person, Vicki and I decided to propose that we share the responsibility. Sometimes I wonder how Vicki ever stumbled on to that job. In our discussions preceding the adventure, Vicki chose to be the efficient office worker and typist while I hoped that my language skills would prove adequate for my portion of the translation.

Thanks to our Parisian boss, lodging had been arranged with a French family living in the suburbs of Paris close to Versailles Castle, the tremendous and historic palace built for Louis XIV. Here, we had planned to recover a couple days from our jet lag. I was far too excited to rest. Almost instantly, I recognized something inside myself that claimed Paris as my true home city. *La Ville Lumière* boasted magnificent monuments, museums, churches, and parks. The city of lights enticed me with its outdoor cafes, student life near the *Sorbonne University,* chic women, art galleries, restaurants, and exquisite architecture. I felt as though I was coming home to the place where I should have been born. Once again, however my blue eyes, blond hair and tall height did not permit me to blend in and appear like a true Parisian. My accent carried too much Chicago nasality in it to pass as a French woman.

Together, we went exploring to search for housing for the summer. I voted for quaintness and in the 6th arrondissement, near *St. Germain Church*, the oldest church in Paris, a rental room was available. Our discovery was a modest hotel without a sculptured façade, but it was near the *Quartier Latin*, the old student quarter. Monsieur had furnished the tiny room with two matching cots and one chair. Our paint-peeling windows overlooked a charming bakery and a produce shop located next door to the butcher where meat hung on racks.

The appearance of raw hanging meat with its stench and swarming flies disgusted me. "Oui," we replied when asked if we chose to rent the room for a total of 85 cents a night. Imagine two, young twenty-one year old women renting a room in Paris for two francs apiece per night. An additional two sous would pay for "la douche," a community shower.

If this job was considered missionary work, then I felt an irresistible urge to go and serve in foreign countries like France. More likely, my calling was the romantic intrigue of Paris. Beginning with the *Musée du Louvre*, a former palace of the kings housing such art treasures as the *Mona Lisa*, the *Winged Victory of Samothrace*, and the *Venus de Milo*, I progressed in concentric circles to familiarize myself with each new quarter. Each evening, we ate ice cream on the tiny streets on the *Ile de la Cité*, the cradle of Paris. Paris was formerly named *Lutèce*, after a tribe called the *Parisii* founded the city on this island, now housing fashionable, antique shops and gourmet cafes.

After work, our routine was to eat in a self-service. Seventy-five cents bought us each a half chicken and some *pommes frites*. After the metro ride from the *Rive Droite* to the *Rive Gauche*, we passed by iron grilled balconies, elegant doorways, mansard roofs, and Frenchmen walking their dogs. The Seine River divides the city into two banks. Vicki and I poured over metro maps and could find where we were going. What a pleasure it was to memorize every smell, sound, and sight in this enchanting city. Strolling through the filtered light in the *Jardin du Luxembourg*, I sat on folded chairs watching children play, birds sing, and flowers bloom in sculptured beds.

One week later, Vicki and I contracted fleas. This situation was embarrassing to explain because the fleas hovered in private places on our bodies and required medical intervention. Self-consciously, we admitted this dilemma to our boss. Upon researching our small boutique hotel, he discovered that we were, in fact, living in a place of ill repute. The frequent nightly knocking on our bedroom door were Algerian workmen who had recently come to Paris. They were searching for more than coffee or French lessons. *"Tant Pis!"* So much the worse! Our boss insisted that we move to a more respectable area.

Within a day, we were happily relocated to a *pension appartement* with a stunning décor that impressed us. The nine-foot windows in our rooms were floor to ceiling and opened outward to an interesting neighborhood. Our double bed was made of brass. Silk drapes covered the windows at night. The wallpaper was a spectacular design of large flowers.

Frugality was hard to maintain. Eating out was tricky since items on the menu didn't always arrive looking like what we thought we ordered. Vicki refused to eat brains. Of course, we always had the choice of eating at the pension. Madame frequently roasted rabbit. Our petit dejeuner arrived on a tray with *chocolat, café au lait,* flaky croissants and teensy dishes filled with fresh butter, cream, and marmalade.

The gift of the summer was exploring a new culture and practicing a new language. My heart delighted in the secrets the city of Paris offered. French people are not bland. *Au Contraire,* they are witty, charming, and brimming with opinions about everything political on the face of the earth. They are renowned for engaging you for hours with their conversation and debates.

Were you to ask me about the job, I can only say that I consider my efforts were paltry. I was ill prepared to translate an evangelical magazine. Nowhere had I learned technical French, which was sorely needed to accomplish the printing of the magazine. Our attempts on the job were accepted graciously. Someone informed me later that Billy Graham had a large number of converts after the Crusade. Crowds thronged to watch him preach the Gospel message.

Late in August, Vicki's brother, Carl, a 2nd lieutenant in the army stationed in Germany and a Wheaton graduate, loaded our luggage and us into his small VW bug. Off we went to travel Western Europe for three more weeks together. *Pas Mal!* Not a bad summer!

We never did make our way to the Billy Graham Crusade.

VII

LEAVING HOME FOR GOOD

"IF YOU INSIST ON GOING to California, then take all of your belongings with you. I am not going to store any of your stuff. Pack up your prom dresses, books, high school annuals, clothes… everything you'll want and need in your life in California. Anything you leave behind, I am planning on taking to the thrift shop on Main Street." These were the harsh words my mother spoke to me in my bedroom two days after returning from Paris.

"Okay, I'll take what I can" was my reply. Under my breath, I muttered something more sarcastic. Mother did not act as though she would miss me.

Looking back now on that decision over forty years ago, I forgive my mother for being so impatient and frustrated that she had so little control over my life now that I was twenty-one years old. My mother went straight into a controlling marriage from her parents' apartment to begin a life with my dad. Thinking about her reaction to me now, I can't help but wonder if she felt some jealousy towards me and intense anger towards my father.

I think he realized that he could not prevent me from discovering my own destiny. He wisely chose not to stop me. Deep inside, I knew this leave taking marked my passage to freedom. With hindsight though, I wish I had said, "Mother, I love you." But I opted to remain silent. Before my aging father dies, I think I'll ask him how much of my decision he understood.

My Storybook doll collection fit into the *American Tourister* luggage. Mary Ellen, my wonderful childhood doll, was left, once again, on my bed. Leaving Mary Ellen behind represented a symbol that I was now an adult woman. She would be safer in the home that she had always known. The next year, I missed Mary Ellen and her comfort.

In the classified ads of the newspaper, I found a woman named Joan who was driving along the same route, U.S. 66, and wanted to share expenses on her trip west.

"Have your bags ready and we'll leave after dinner," she responded after we made arrangements on the telephone. We began the trip to the West Coast in her 1955 Chevy. Her plans became delayed and it was close to midnight when we actually departed. What Joan never stated was her expectation that we would not only share gasoline costs, but that I would take over half of the driving responsibility to our destination point in Oklahoma. This adventure was a straight-through drive.

My parents looked angry and bewildered when we drove off into the night. This dilemma could have been resolved had I bothered to inform her that not only did I not possess a driver's license, but I had never driven anything except a Schwinn bicycle. What I did not bother to inform her was that my single experience behind a driver's wheel resulted in my yanking the gearshift knob off my dad's English Ford, and he suspended my driving lessons as some form of retribution.

Joan persisted that this was our understood agreement so I drove. Nine hundred miles behind the wheel of a stick shift car taught me invaluable driving lessons. Our route took us from Western Springs, Illinois to Ft. Cobb, Oklahoma—just another lesson in independence that left me with very sweaty palms and the tightness of fear in my throat. Mountains and fog accompanied us on that excursion. I did not elaborate on my personal terror to the driver. Joan slept much of the trip.

Upon arrival at my grandmother's modest home in Oklahoma, Mother Gracie stuffed the driver and me with home baked cookies and pies, fried chicken and mashed potatoes and lime green gelatin salad. Miniature marshmallows floated in the Jello salad. She had picked Swiss chard from her vegetable garden and steamed it in her pressure cooker. After lunch, the driver, Joan, said farewell and left. We did not exchange telephone numbers. This trip was officially ended.

Mother Gracie and I spent a sleepy afternoon rocking in wicker chairs on her porch, chatting and dozing. Occasionally we flipped through the pages of some old photo albums. Out popped the handsome faces of her deceased husband, Ralph, her deceased son, Robert, and her daughter, my mother, Dorothy Grace. Included in those photos were pictures of her two sisters and one brother. Her closeness to her siblings resulted in a family reunion with them each August.

Mother Gracie and her sister Annie had married two Gooderl brothers from Kansas and they always lived close to each other. Annie delivered a stillborn child at birth. After Annie died, my parents advised my grandmother to move from Illinois to Oklahoma to be near her surviving sister. Aunt Cynthia impressed me as being a somewhat rigid old lady, but the two sisters enjoyed each other enormously. Aunt Cynthia didn't laugh much. For two days, I caught up on news with Mother Gracie and then it was time to leave. With some hesitation, I said goodbye. My personality and temperament were much more in sync with my Grandmother than with my mother. My grandmother knew instinctively how to have fun. She dressed up for every day and tinted her hair a bluish color.

Furthermore, she believed that everyone ought to eat apple pie for breakfast. *Dignified* women like my grandmother wore girdles and flower-patterned house dresses. I knew that she was the adult whom I would miss. I found it difficult to leave the comfort of her four-poster bed. She sent me off with a hug and a box of homemade brownies.

The airplane departed. A thousand questions popped into my head during that flight. *How would I survive by myself?* I went into the plane lavatory and smoked a cigarette. *What did I think I was doing leaving home?* Regardless, I was finally free. No one would be there to insist I do something against my will. *Would the girl I met on the ferry crossing the English Channel really pick me up at the airport? How does one rent an apartment?*

Incessant questions cluttered my mind and I started to feel some apprehension. *Why did my father insist in charging me 6% interest on the $600.00 loan to get me started? What would West Covina High School be like? Did I actually want to be a teacher? Was I capable or just plain stupid? Whatever happened to my desire to be a missionary in Africa? Why was there no skyline of Los Angeles when the plane landed?* I saw mountains and the Pacific Ocean, but no skyscrapers. *Why did the air appear brown and make my eyes sting?*

Confused, I developed a throbbing headache. A relentless, emotional ping-pong game seemed to fill up all the space where my brain had been. Barbara, the woman I met on the ferryboat to England, was there to meet the plane. On the way to the parking lot, juggling luggage and boxes, we chatted. Instantaneous relief came over me, appreciating that she had not forgotten to meet my airplane.

An invitation was extended to stay in her aunt's home with her for three days while I became oriented to the unfamiliar situation. That night, surrounded by boxes and my dependable *American Tourister* luggage, I climbed into a strange bed feeling lonely. Then I began to cry. Loneliness cut deep into my heart that sleepless night. I forgot to talk to Jesus because I thought I was now independent. How I wish my plastic night light of Jesus had been mounted on the bedroom wall. Mary Ellen would have whispered reassurance in my ear.

Part of the adventure as well as the mounting anxiety was about having insufficient data regarding the teaching position. Orientation began. Within the first hour, I spotted a pretty, brown-haired woman who also was beginning her first assignment and I introduced myself. Her name was Kay Lemasters, and she introduced me to her seatmate, Lucille Yoshimoto. By lunchtime, we were bonding.

Kay described her background as Midwestern and conservative. I heard about her life in the teacher's cafeteria where we had a cigarette. I was happy that someone who was attractive and interesting sought me out. After all the tedious meetings, it was lunchtime. Inside, I felt another kind of hunger that a hamburger would not fill. I was ravenous for comforting words and reassurance about this wild decision.

Guilt crept into my mind as I recalled defying my parents' wishes. Although I very much wanted to honor my folks' desires, my heart had already decided at age fifteen that I would come to California. I knew this reality to be my destiny.

By afternoon, Lucille, Kay, and I agreed to go apartment hunting and sign a one-year lease. The principal of our school, Mr. Maurice Wooden, offered to help us on our search. Patiently, he drove us up and down Azusa Avenue. There we checked out several, furnished apartments. Our one requirement was to have a swimming pool situated in the center of the complex surrounded by Palm trees. The trees would look good in our photos that we would send home. By dinnertime, we were signing our names to a rental agreement. I won the coin toss for not sharing a bedroom, which meant that I would pay extra rent for a single room.

The three of us moved in the following day. We all bought new towels and sheets, food and a goldfish bowl. Setting up a household for Lucille meant that she never unpacked her boxes. For an entire year, a tower of boxes stood in the living room corner obstructing the view to the kitchen where unwashed dishes sat soaking in the sink. Occasionally, trash spilled out onto the floor. Not one of us obsessed about cleaning. A memory we all shared were comments from visitors wondering why dead goldfish floated on top of the brackish water in the bowl on top of the coffee table.

The teaching contract specified a beginning salary as $5,200.00 per year, paid in ten monthly checks. To me, this amount of money was a fortune. My children laugh to think that I lived on five hundred dollars a month. I opened a checking account and learned how to balance the checkbook. It seemed like there was so much to learn about surviving in the adult world.

Terror gripped my shaking voice the first day of school. Mini skirts were the fashion and I owned six teaching outfits. There were some eighteen-year-old boys in my homeroom. *Was I some sort of fraud trying to pass myself off as a teacher? Was this false arrogance that I might be able to teach something to these adolescents?*

"Mesdemoiselles et messieurs: nous allons apprehendre la langue française," I spoke to them in French and informed them we would learn French together. The

French language has a musical quality with its rising and falling intonation and soft endings. My goals were to immerse them in the sounds before they looked at the written word. Any language instructor will confirm this as an effective teaching tool.

*Voici Monsieur Thibaut et Voila Madame Thibaut
ils sont à la maison. Répétez, s'il vous plaît.*

The Thibaults are at home. Repeat, please.

In chorus, they responded. I liked my students and they, in turn, challenged themselves to repeat and practice. They trusted me not to embarrass their efforts and class was fun.

Exhausted by 4:00 PM, Kay, Lucille and I were driven back to our apartment where we crashed on our beds until one of us mentioned food. Meal preparation became a problem since Kay and I had never learned to cook and Lucille kept a stash of seaweed rice under the sink, which looked disgusting. Several nights a week, we visited the International House of Pancakes. Our reasoning followed the premise that we should eat at an international restaurant because we were all teaching languages. Lucille was Asian from Hawaii and she taught Spanish. Kay came from Ohio and taught English. Our other bonding habit was smoking cigarettes. We thought this made us appear quite sophisticated. We all smoked Marlboros.

Gradually, we each learned how to exercise some control over our first year of teaching anxiety. Looking back, I am amazed how diligently we prepared our lesson plans that we turned in weekly to our department chairperson. West Covina High School was preparing for an accreditation review.

That first year of teaching was so instructive. Watching adolescents learn was rewarding. Gaining the respect of older teachers reinforced my work ethic. Correcting papers filled our weekends. Despite the times of bewilderment and frustration, our ambitious endeavors proved personally rewarding.

With the exception of our lazy food preparation, the three of us took pleasure in our living arrangement. Toward the end of the academic year, I had mastered the preparation of macaroni and cheese, which was an improvement from eating ice cream out of the container and smearing peanut butter on top of that as my dinner. We were managing to act like grown-up adults.

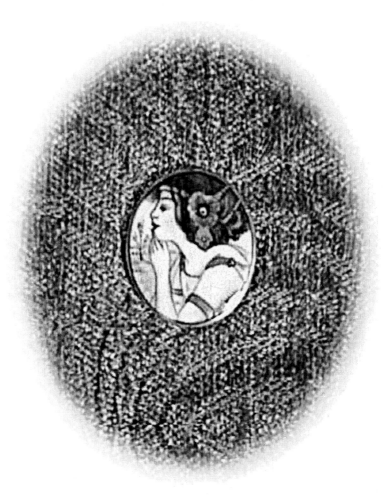

VIII

THE LANGUAGE OF LOVE:
CATCH A RISING STAR

SOMETIME IN OCTOBER 1963, the telephone rang one evening in my apartment, and my college-roommate, Grace, mentioned an idea to organize a reunion soon. Grace's Wheaton College degree in philosophy was first utilized working in Juvenile Hall. Helping children who were being detained was the first position she discovered after her relocation to the West Coast. Neither of us owned or had access to cars. There was no public transportation between West Covina and Brentwood where she lived. Grace devised an idea for us to have a double date. Freddy Schmitka, a Gallo wine salesman, agreed to come out to West Covina and pick me up and drive me to Grace's apartment. Then the three of us would wait and have a drink until my blind date, Steve, arrived from his job. This would be another first experience in my life—a blind date.

"Would you take a risk and go out once with Freddy's roommate?" Grace asked.

"Sure, I think it would be fun," I replied. "Tell me what you know about him."

"Well, he's supposed to be blond with a crew cut and he's a film actor."

"A film actor, hmmm..."

I still don't know why Grace was seeing Freddy when we all knew the real reason she had come to California was to snare up her former boyfriend, Jack, who had been expelled from Wheaton College for smoking on the fire escape stairs and was now enrolled at UCLA Grace had been in love with Jack for almost three years.

Freddy arrived the evening of the date and blew the car horn loudly.

"What should I do now if he doesn't come to the front door?" I asked roommate Kay not knowing if this was polite. I felt quite nervous getting picked up like that without my folks meeting the guy. Freddy turned out be very easy-going and friendly. The drive on the freeways lasted two hours, and I learned more than I needed to know about wine salesmen. Freddy explained the whole process of winemaking and told me what gave Gallo wine its distinctive flavor and aroma. Frankly, I didn't care. I was too nervous about the blind date.

Upon arriving at Grace's penthouse apartment, we discovered her blending a dressing for the Caesar salad.

"When had Grace learned how to cook?" I asked her. Smiling, she dropped in a raw egg and whipped the ingredients all together, garnishing the top with shaved cheese and anchovies. It was also the first time that I had seen a Jewish guy pop a wine cork. The Schwartz's drank a Jewish port to celebrate. Freddy had brought a large jug of red wine to the dinner party. An hour later, an apologetic Steve knocked on the door, Dressed in khaki pants and a madras shirt with a short crew cut, he looked really handsome.

"Hi, I've been eager to meet you. You must be Steve Galton," I said, beginning the conversation a little nervously. Steve smiled a warm smile but did not engage in eye contact. Actually, I was unaccustomed to shy men and so I just began non-stop babbling about the summer in Paris. I think he may have been uncomfortable with a monologue about Europe.

"Sorry, I had to work late," Steve explained why he missed most of the dinner hour.

"That's okay. What do you do?" I asked.

"I fill vending machines over at UCLA and I attend classes part time."

"Grace told me that you are a movie star. Is that true?"

"Gosh not exactly. I got hired on as an extra in the film *Spartacus*. You can spot me because I forgot to remove my Elgin wrist watch."

I laughed until I howled. Something so endearing and familiar fills up my heart whenever I recall this first meeting. I married him, because his first words to me acknowledged his honest and good character. His very first words to me demanded my heart. Memories of that night remain softly on a shelf somewhere inside me. *This is an intriguing and modest man who is in addition handsome and intelligent*, I thought.

There was nothing then but love, a wondering of what would happen if I gave my heart to him. This was a man to whom I felt unreserved attraction. *Moon River* played on the car radio, and later we stopped by a roadside bar in Malibu to dance. Steve told Freddy that he would take me home. That night, I am convinced, divine help arrived when Steve drove me home to West Covina at 2:00 AM.

"May I kiss you goodnight?" asked Steve.

All the stifling loneliness and self-sufficiency, I guarded as my defenses for being rejected, melted. It seemed as though the night air was filled with honey. I reached up for his embrace and felt a collaboration in that first kiss that we would be with each other forever. From that first date, I have admired and respected him.

A second date, ten days later, took us to Tijuana to witness Jai Lai games in some filthy bar. Jai Lai games are some kind of indoor racket ball. I hesitated in sitting down in the bar on account of the filth. I don't know why Steve thought that would be fun. Nothing about that border town interested me. As we were about to leave, someone vomited all over my new pleated, trench coat. Steve's Hillman car reeked of this foul odor all the way home.

A dense fog prevented any visibility on the exhausting drive back to Los Angeles and we didn't arrive at my place until 3:00 AM. Despite the evening going less well than anticipated, I remember being so happy to be with him. I began to hope that we would have a future dating relationship.

One of the most endearing attributes about Steve is how reserved he is. People always trust him to be fair and unassuming. Family history had taught me about aggressive men who always insist on being in control. I did wonder why Steve was not more emotionally available. You see, I was in love and wanted to be with him forever. Steve was not concerned about being a loner. What others say behind his back is always positive. He confided in me that his father had died in a tragic accident when he was barely two years old. His mother was hospitalized for over six months and dominant controlling women raised him during that ordeal. I learned that there was an emotional distance in his family. No one had been present to guide him either. Steve had attended various colleges and carried the disappointment that he, for financial reasons, could not attend the Air Force Academy. My husband graduated as the valedictorian of his high school and possesses a brilliant and curious mind.

Steve has a sister, named Rosann, who is two years older. She held her brother's hand, at the scene of the accident, for hours until the police discovered the distressing situation of two children wandering by the side of a road. Decades later, I am sorry that we were never in close geographical proximity to form an intimate friendship with his sister. Rosann is married to Cameron, her college sweetheart, and they had three children. All the children have followed in the faith-filled footsteps of their parents. Rosann is interested in a variety of hobbies, and like her brother, is genuinely kind.

While I had begun to speak the language of love with this man whom I adored, Steve began to open up some of the challenges he had confronted in his college studies. His ultimate dream was to join the Foreign Service, and he had passed one part of the exam and qualified for a top security clearance. One hurdle that continued to be bothersome was his apparent difficulty in learning a foreign language fluently enough to speak it. This would be essential were he to pursue his goal. A two-year stint in the army had further delayed his completion of a college degree. Steve admitted that he had struggled with French twice and received a "D" grade. Perhaps, that is the most convincing reason that he was interested in me.

How surprised I was to discover my obsession with this man. The urge to pursue him intensified and I became absorbed in his world and wanted to attract his attention. I found myself telephoning him and feeling jealous whenever he planned activities without me.

Our third date was scheduled for the afternoon of November 22nd, 1963. En route to UCLA, our designated meeting spot, I heard on the radio that John Kennedy had been shot. Students walked across the almost empty campus sobbing. Apprehensively, I waited forty-five minutes after our appointed time when finally a red-eyed Steve appeared in front of Royce Hall.

"I didn't think you would wait for me," he apologized. Fragile and shocked, we spent the entire weekend in front of the television in his apartment watching the news and feeling the horror of the nation's tragedy. Steve was an ardent Kennedy supporter and a Democrat. Up to that point, I displayed no interest in political life.

I was absolutely stunned. Life was instantly splintered and a certain child-like trust evaporated throughout the nation on that long, horrifying weekend.

By Monday morning, my feelings for Steve were sufficiently aroused, and I somewhat convinced myself that I could coerce him into feeling as intimately about me. I craved emotional closeness—Steve, on the other end of the emotional spectrum, was fearful of my intensity and chose to remain fairly self-contained. I interpreted his attitude to mean that I was not as desirable as I hoped concerning our future. I kept waiting for him to say that he was sorry, but that he had met someone else.

Love is coming, I tried to reassure myself. I was searching for a man who could give of himself totally. Then, I persisted without the conscious knowledge of my personal neediness. *Please love me and nurture me*, I silently begged.

Months passed by and we continued to date. A sense of panic overwhelmed me, fearing that I would be unable to find a suitable marriage partner before my twenty-second birthday and I risked remaining an "old maid." A family might start if Steve would only fall in love with me. In my silent daydreaming, I planned our life.

During this period of turmoil, Steve began to make plans to return to school and finally acquire his degree in Economics.

"I want to complete my educational goals," he insisted.

"It's simple," I told him. "You just concentrate on designing a plan for your life, and then pursue your dreams," I advised. "Tell me something about your future that you aspire to accomplish."

The bombardment commenced. Understanding, affection, and advice were offered unsolicited. Yes, I wanted this man and I thought I would prevail if only he became dependent on me. Such manipulation could only destroy the genuine basis of love between us. I wanted this man, this opposite counterpart, to fulfill the empty, void places within me. Obviously, any insightful person can recognize the absurdity of my forced engulfment. Steve is a patient man in life's important choices and he stood by me. Not long ago, Steve confided that he wasn't emotionally ready to marry so young.

Our courtship sustained some turbulent and treacherous times as well as some bright and hopeful aspirations. In the interval between certainty and the not knowing, we took the great risk to commit ourselves to a lifetime journey together.

"You are being impulsive as usual," my father warned me. "Your mother and I don't know anything about him and he hasn't finished college. Why can't you find a man who has a completed education and a responsible career?" My parents didn't meet Steve until two days before our wedding. The introduction was a disaster waiting to happen. My dad never ceased grilling him with questions. I wouldn't want my daughter to be as insistent without consulting me, but she will still have to figure out how to have a marriage based on her own desires. Mark and Shelby shared a fairy tale, and I remain forever grateful that those two souls met and loved. Destiny is a part of life, and courage moves us onward to the uncertain.

So, our courtship continued for nine months. With my childhood Baptist minister, Dr. I.C. Peterson officiating at the service in a Methodist church in Western Springs, Illinois, Steve and I exchanged traditional vows and began our life together on August 15th, 1964.

"You will be married in an air-conditioned church, at the very least," my mother once again prevailed. "You cannot be married outdoors or have violin music," she insisted.

I liked my simple A-line wedding gown and blusher veil. Nothing exceptional happened during the service except my father stepped on my train giving me away and everyone in the church gasped when they heard the rip of the satin train. Our reception was held in the church parlor where guests drank sherbet punch and ate nuts, pastel mints, and wedding cake. There was no champagne at the reception. Dr. Peterson handed us a brown wrapper paper book after our one counseling session, which I guess was supposed to answer all the questions we might encounter about our sexual relationship. That was altogether a different era, with expectations that would seem unrealistic to young couples today.

Three hours later, Steve and I arrived at the Drake Hotel for our honeymoon night. Grace was my maid of honor and Steve's best friend from childhood, Bob Spencer, served him as best man. Bob brought a bottle of champagne to our room, which the four of us shared.

"I expect you both to be here for an 8:00 AM breakfast tomorrow morning," my mother demanded firmly before we left in our going-away clothes. Still in my backroom closet hangs the navy suit that I wore. Since I was wearing white gloves, Steve pinned a gardenia corsage on my collar. I remember the adrenaline rush.

By noon, the following day, we were packed and in our rental Cadillac car headed for a three-day cross-country honeymoon back to California. Both the journey across the desert and the lifetime marital journey have provided inspiring scenery. In addition, we have witnessed some arid landscapes, which served as backdrops for the Galton family history.

Intimacy is a life long process. Steve and I are grateful for our decision to marry. Perseverance and mutual respect, in addition to stubbornness, have paved our path together. I give thanks that our footsteps have been side by side.

IX

DISCOVERING THE WORLD TOGETHER: CREATING A LIFE WITH STEVE

UPON OUR RETURN FROM OUR WEDDING, we settled into a two bedroom, furnished apartment in Arcadia. Playing house and learning how to cook became instant hobbies. Steve flattered all my efforts in the kitchen, which bolstered my confidence. Especially on the occasions when—in front of company—I had dropped the meat loaf on the kitchen floor. Scooping up the meatloaf, we set it back on the platter and served our guests.

We shared what little we had accumulated. Steve brought a great record collection to the marriage and the only piece of furniture we purchased was a Spinet piano on which I played my eighth grade recital piece, *Rustle of Spring*.

During the weekdays I taught, and at night I worked on acquiring a life teaching credential. To keep Steve confident while he successfully passed his language requirement, I accompanied him to his German class at

USC. While never a lover of language, Steve preferred the orderly structure of German and we treated ourselves to hamburgers in the Student Union.

Each of us felt a sense of excitement, that Steve would be earning his bachelor's degree that June. But a surprise awaited me.

"Grace, what would you think of my attending law school?" Steve casually inquired as we sat sipping root beer and munching on burgers at the A&W drive-through restaurant on Rosemead Avenue.

"Why would you want to do that if we are going into the Foreign Service?" I asked.

"Well, I have been thinking that law might be a better field for me to enter."

In August 1966, Steve and I drove our shiny, new black VW bug back to Michigan to visit my parents at their summer home on Bass Lake. I remember my younger brother, David being in overt conflict with my father. Steve begged to leave after the first mealtime.

"Your family is crazy," he stated.

Years later in graduate school studying psychology, I learned the language of family systems and about the roles family members unconsciously agree to play. I completed an exercise that I appropriately named *The Feeding*. In this collage, I described my family of origin with bird symbols. I tried to imagine the various family members as the birds that walk on water. I cut out pictures of birds and glued them onto a piece of butcher paper sitting around a table I had drawn.

Steve was the one who sat on Mother's left and I called her The Vulture. At age 56, she appeared rapacious, subsisted on prey that she destroyed and then fed on their dead carcasses. Most everybody felt deadness or the sensation of being chewed up after an encounter with her.

Steve, I referred to as the Roadrunner bird. "Meep meep. We're hitting the road back to California. Your family is crazy. Meep."

I called my youngest brother, Scott, the Dove because he avoided all conflict and only discussed safe topics like sports or school. "Let me tell you about that tennis match," he cooed.

I described myself as the Bird In Fight. "I wanted to be here for this reunion but maybe, I really don't" I squawked.

Brother Bob was then age 26 and he became the Spruce Goose. "I'm busy raising a family, being cool, becoming a millionaire," He said spreading his feathers.

Dad, I identified as the Western Grebe. Grebes have long necks and stick their neck into every thing. "We'll settle this in the other room," he shouted to David. "You will do what I say!" Whack... bang... slap. Once the fight was over, Dad returned to the table, shirt torn, face bloodied, and said, "David, return thanks and say the blessing."

David served as The Decoy. At age 17, he absorbed most of the family conflict and had already grown into a six-foot eight-inch tall bully. "You're a jerk!" he once told my father. "You can't tell me what to do anymore." After the violent, bloody fight took place in the bedroom, the birds sat at the table as though nothing unusual had occurred. Furniture had even been broken. Steve and I once took Scott, who had been sitting on the front doorstop crying, in our car over to a deserted road and Steve taught Scott how to drive a stick shift. The Dove has always tried hard to be good, distract people from anger, make peace in a safe way, and protect himself from further injury. The Dove and the Roadrunner have remained trusted and respectful friends.

For our second wedding anniversary, I gave Steve a legal dictionary and he gave me roses. We returned to California when an offer came unsolicited to rent our aunt's home in Silver Lake for the three years of law school. We quickly accepted her offer and moved. Auntie got married for the first time at age 50. Auntie was Steve's father's youngest sister and she had been Los Angeles' first female police sergeant and former president of the Sierra Club. Steve and I attended her wedding ceremony and Steve walked her down the aisle. Auntie Mary and her husband, Noel, moved to Northern California. Her one failure was in taking me on a camping trip, which I detested. She described pouring down rain as a "misty evening."

For months, we had debated the topic of whether to move to northern California.

"I just love the city of San Francisco," I begged.

"You'll have to teach wherever I get accepted to law school," I was informed. This topic bounced around for quite awhile and our decision was made after Steve was accepted at USC School of Law.

Steve chose mainly day classes. At orientation, an arrogant law professor barked at the student body.

"Look to the left and look to the right. One of you won't be sitting here next year."

"Wow! That was scary." I whispered to Steve. "That is a mighty high attrition rate."

Law school took up all Steve's time and energy for three years. You would either see him studying or on a typewriter. We took out a large student loan to pay tuition. Sometimes, Steve's mother, Marie encouraged her son by helping out with the expense of textbooks.

Meanwhile, I obtained my teaching credential and switched high schools. To my surprise, a member of WASC, a California based accreditation team approached me with an offer. This gentleman visited two of my French classes.

"Listen, Mrs. Galton, if you ever consider changing high schools, give us a call. We would be interested in interviewing you."

"Steve, it makes good sense to teach at a school which carries more prestige." I argued.

"I don't want you teaching in any politically conservative, right wing school district," he replied adamantly.

Debates ensued. Eventually after a successful interview, Steve agreed that La Canada High School was indeed a prestigious teaching environment. Today, the district test scores rank second in southern California. At the same time, Steve was cramming new facts and information into his mind; I unpacked my teaching files and prepared my classroom ambiance.

Forty per cent of the faculty was new. The campus was only two years old. Teaching French was rewarding and I was surprised that so many students were actually learning the language. So, I was not the fraud I feared myself to be. Conviviality reigned. Every Friday night, we either attended a high school football game or attended numerous faculty parties. If I worked in the food booth at a game, I could earn an extra twenty-five dollars. Monitoring standardized tests also brought in additional money. Steve and I exercised a high level of personal discipline during that time in our marriage. Nothing obscured our vision to achieve our academic goals. We both strived to succeed in our endeavors.

Summers were different and we took a break. Finally, Steve wanted to see Western Europe with me. For our expenses to be paid, we would have to act as chaperones for sixteen students I recruited from La Canada and West Covina High Schools. Our own group was connected to a larger study and travel program. What an adventure! The summer of 1967, we studied French at the University of Strasbourg and then spent three weeks traveling. Steve was hooked and hasn't ever regretted having a travel bag ready to go. The following summer, we chose another travel opportunity, and chaperoned nineteen students.

In an old scrapbook that I located in the garage, I found a ripped, worn, newspaper article written in 1967. The Glendale News Press reported:

It's not the going that counts—it's what you do when you get there. And students from La Canada High School, who traveled to Europe last summer under a program sponsored by the American Institute for Foreign Study, did a lot. Education and travel were combined under the unique program. Fun was another ingredient added to the eight weeks abroad. When you travel with chaperones like Mr. and Mrs. Steve Galton, who also organized the trip, you can count on getting the most out of a vacation, according to the students. The Galtons' enthusiasm and energy are contagious. Included in the six-week program was a month's study at the University at Strasbourg.

"You really learn a language," said Kim LaValley who majored in French. "You speak it all the time and develop a real interest in it and the French people." The students lived in dormitories on the campus and on the weekends took side trips. At the conclusion of the program, diplomas were awarded

"You really learn to know yourself on a trip like this," said Amy Inge. "You learn to give a little and be patient. The most fun was meeting new people with different ideas and different customs than ours." The trip sparked wanderlust in the students and all want to go again. Many have decided to study abroad for one or two years during college. And go again they may! The Galtons are organizing another trip. This time under the auspices of the Foreign Study League, the vacation will combine travel with a comparative study of the political institutions, personalities and trends of the countries visited."

"We will take twenty high school students from La Canada, Glendale, San Marino, and Pasadena," said Mrs. Galton naming the departure date as June 17. The trip will include ten days each in Rome, Geneva, Paris and London, with side trips to Oxford, Stratford on Avon, Versailles, Naples, Pompeii and the Swiss Alps. Students will be granted an audience with Pope Paul and will visit with other high-ranking dignitaries."

At the conclusion of the first trip, we received a letter and check from the American Institute for Foreign Study. The letter stated:

Enclosed please find our check for $214.80, which represents payment to you for your services this summer as teacher-chaperone on our Summer School in Europe Program.

We were ecstatic to receive so much money for having such a wonderful time.

I do believe Steve and I could have done that forever. Upon arrival home, I learned, to my sheer delight that we had conceived a baby, probably in a castle in Germany. By the spring of 1969, we would be proud parents. Steve would be a lawyer by the following summer. Life was wonderful. Our life plan was progressing successfully and we were on target, I thought.

X

REMARKABLE MARK:
MAN OF COURAGE

FOLLOWING AN EXCITING nine-month pregnancy, Mark Stephen entered the world on May 6th, 1969 at 9:28 AM on a cloudy Tuesday morning. Students had watched him wiggle and stretch for months, as I continued to sit on a stool in my classroom trying to teach French, but I often felt exhausted by the strong, muscular movements he made. As I continued to bulge out, Mark appeared to be practicing somersaults on his way to his birthing day. News of his birth was posted on the school marquis. Excited students came to visit us in the hospital.

We brought him home from Glendale Memorial Hospital on Mother's Day weekend. He was dressed in a tiny blue and white-striped suit with matching visor cap. Steve and I were ecstatic to hold this brand new baby son. Gratitude spilled from our hearts as we looked at his beautiful face. He immediately began screaming with colic for three months. Steve was in the waiting room and not actually present for the actual birth. I well remember my first words to Mark and Steve:

101

It's a little boy. Hi little Mark.
We have waited so long for you!

Tears streamed down my face this morning when I read that greeting in his baby book. The Latin teacher sent a telegram congratulating Mark on his fine choice of parents. As a new, inexperienced mother, I was vigilant in wanting to protect him from all harm—from scraped knees to bruised feelings. How I ache to protect him again. I simply want to touch that blond hair, and look into his intense, blue eyes, and laugh again with him. Mark's cheery face caused everyone to smile back at him. Then, he liked to clap his hands, as though he was offering himself applause.

Aspects of Mark's personality stood out prominently from the very first month of his emerging development. Instantly, we recognized that he preferred making noise to being silent. Throughout his life, he preferred being around people to being alone. The age of his companions made no difference. Mark, always, protested loudly when he was not satisfied. His temperament was arranged in such a manner that he focused on continually attempting new paths in life. Both on a physical and emotional plane, he hiked and blazed new and unfamiliar trails, dragging the family behind him.

Nocturnal rides in our VW settled his colicky evenings. Never had I witnessed anybody so anxious to get going in the morning. Laughing, with his arms outstretched, Mark resisted staying in bed after 6:00 AM. Some quality in him made him always want to be moving, whether that meant jumping off a precarious perch on the dresser into our arms, playing in his sand box in the back yard, or riding on his tiny tricycle. Once, I discovered Mark sitting in front of the open refrigerator tossing a dozen raw eggs on the floor—one by one—just to see what would happen to them. Another afternoon, during naptime, Mark took off his soiled diaper and decided to sponge paint his bedroom walls. Mark became an expressive, little boy. His first speech centered on action words: "go-go" for car and "up-up" for play.

When he cried too hard, which was normally at a sleep time, I settled him in his plastic, orange and green infant seat on top of the clothes dryer to console him. That was probably dangerous, but the motion of the dryer calmed him and slowed him down. In fact, all his life, Mark preferred active motion and vigorous physical activity. As I gaze upon a staggering number of photos in albums and in shoeboxes, I find only one shot of Mark in repose. There, he rests on Humpty Dumpty in his crib.

Mark was born the year that Neil Armstrong first walked on the moon. I wouldn't have been surprised if he had beaten him to it. We all would comment that Mark chose living life to the most thrilling possibilities. He left a trail of friends and laughter. Mark's active imagination inspired creative adventures, and he investigated what was in every drawer and cabinet and usually applied the product to his body.

Brad arrived in our family sixteen months later. These two little blond boys were inseparable for years. They played outdoors under the trees or in them—a stick in each hand—rolling over rocks, looking for insects, jumping off boulders, daring each other to invent another fun activity. Visiting overnight at Grandma Marie's house was wonderful fun for them, and she patiently allowed them to track their muddy footprints all over her laundry room, without scolding them.

Playing Cowboys and Indians was Mark's favorite game theme. Often, he pointed either the arrow or the pistol at his little brother. Mark's gestures as a child were always about play. Neighbor children sought him out each morning. Sometimes, Mark got so filthy playing outside that we simply hosed him down before he was allowed into the house. He learned early to peel off his clothes and leave his bug collection outside.

Mark taught us all how to be playful. Photos remind us of fishing in Michigan, taking road trips up the coast, building forts, bringing flowers to new teachers, drawing pictures, making books at school, and taking bubble baths with brother, Brad. There were tree houses in the backyard where the neighbor children played. Mark once cut off the limbs of some tall pine trees to make tree forts.

"Mark, did you really saw off the branches of the pine trees?"

"Yes, mom, I thought they would just grow back."

Lemonade became popular back in the canyon area. Many of the boys in the neighborhood brought adult magazines to the fort to peruse. Someone mentioned to me that my Lenox fine china was used in the fort one day for a hot dog meal. Mark then organized a game of Frisbee with my bread and butter plates. It wasn't until the next Thanksgiving that I realized six plates were missing.

Mark wrote poems at school. They were usually short and to the point. Because he was crazy about sports, the theme in the poem usually included some concept of competition.

Baseball

Baseball is fun,
Baseball is great.
We like baseball.
So play it until late.

Teachers were carefully observing his short attention span in class. Attention deficit disorder was being monitored. Our pediatrician treated Mark's hyperactivity with medication, but he continued on with enormous energy. Some of this unleashed energy went into sports.

Here's Mark's poem, composed after he took up competitive swimming at age five or six:

Swimming

Do you like to swim at a pool?
Do you like to win at a meet?
Any one would be a fool
To want to experience defeat.

Mark's imagination knew no limits. At age eight, he wrote and illustrated a book. Included in the contents are visits to the circus, an imaginary jet ride, and adventures parachuting down to dinosaur land. He wrote about watching a volcano go off before venturing down to the sea to visit the sharks that were golfing. Later, landing on the moon, Mark spotted a space creature that chased him back to the rocket ship.

Sifting through another box of pictures, I discovered a photo showing Mark carefully holding his baby sister, Lissy, on her Baptism day. Mark would have been ten years old. Brad and Jeremy, his younger brothers, are also sitting in front of the fireplace. This photo dazzles me and conjures up those feelings that all my children were my favorites.

Raising children humbles a parent. Each child has a distinct personality and must be treated accordingly. Once again, I threw myself back into the hands of God and pleaded for guidance in my parenting skills. There had been deficiencies in my upbringing, and I knew that I was passing on what I observed as a child. We joined the La Canada Presbyterian Church. Through a couple's group, we met a fine group of friends. Soon, we were involved in a variety of activities at the church and it became a nurturing faith home while our children grew to maturity.

Each child was baptized there. The sacrament of Baptism is the reminder our children belong ultimately to God and not to us. I made my choice to be baptized at age eight, and I publicly acknowledged that I trusted God to accompany me through life. Even then, I knew my name was written on the palm of God's hand. Four children were a rich blessing from God. I wanted them all to be baptized as babies to demonstrate that Steve and I would raise them in the church and introduce them to their Creator. Our children's baptismal days are unique markers in my life. Mark Stephen Galton was baptized on October 19, 1969.

And so, it appeared that Mark was born for success. "You can do what you want to do today," became his motto. He achieved at all sports, preferring water polo and becoming team captain as well as achieving success, winning the Rio Hondo league championship. Mark was an avid skier, hiker, mountain biker, and golfer. Nothing intimidated him in the water from sailing to scuba diving.

Mark cared deeply about people and offered care and compassion to older folks. Frequently, at social events, he chose to speak personally to the elderly before he engaged his peers.

After considering many colleges, Mark chose to receive his Bachelor of Arts degree in communications from the University of Southern California where he was active with Sigma Chi fraternity. A tiny tattoo on his ankle reminds us of his identification with Sigma Chi. For two consecutive years, Mark's handsome face adorned the school calendar. In my opinion, Mark was majoring mostly in fun during those undergraduate years.

Later, in the year 2000, he earned a master's degree in Business Administration in Informational Technology from USC's Marshall School of Business. Until his illness, Mark was employed as a senior consultant for KPMG consulting firm, now known as Bearing Point in its media practice.

One of Mark's favorite songs is *Into the Mystic*, by Van Morrison. The lyrics are lulling:

We were born before the wind.
Ah, so younger than the sun.
And the bonnie boat was one
as we sailed into the mystic.

Mark is now into the mysterious mystic. He has smelled the sea and felt the sky. His soul has inspired me and continues to touch many lives as people hear his story. As the song reminds me, *When the foghorn blows, I will be coming home.* Mark is safely home and returns to us daily in our fondest memories.

I tried to capture my own feelings in a poem for him:

Man of Courage

Son, oh precious son, child of blessing, heir of promise,
This is a memory day and my heart aches for you.

Son of love, our love's expression,
Eager young man with energy to burn,
You followed joy, and lead us to laughter.

We talk of you and how you made your life extraordinary.
We listen to the songs you knew.
We hike the trails of life and nature
And we remember that you loved whatever you were doing.

You left the legacy of faithful son and loving brother.
To your wife, there was never any other.

When did you face your own mortality?
So many things we still want to say,
I wonder when you stumbled from health to sickness,
Did you know your life would be a short one?
We know you would soar back if you could find a way,
So send us yellow birds to cheer us for we cannot see beyond.

Child of love, journey in love's way
And meet us at the wide horizon with the setting sun.

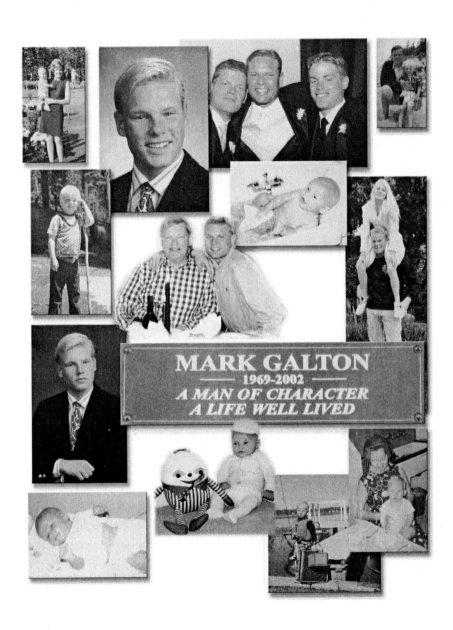

MARK GALTON
—— 1969-2002 ——
A MAN OF CHARACTER
A LIFE WELL LIVED

XI

THE LANGUAGE OF COMMUNITY:
CREATING BONDS

RAISING TWO LITTLE BOYS together, barely sixteen months apart, required physical stamina as well as patience. Each night, after tucking them into their cribs, I was only too ready to enjoy some adult companionship. My husband Steve's profession, as a city attorney, required his attendance at several city council meetings per week spread over the San Gabriel valley. These cities were situated some distance from our apartment and we owned only one car. Many hours of each day were spent running after two toddlers. Physical fitness came from bending down to lift up smudged little bodies and kissing their smiling faces. In the evening hours, we all felt like whining from exhaustion.

Our apartment only had a tiny plot of grass where the boys could ride their tiny self-propelled coasters. The most cherished thoughts that I hold close to my heart are of absolute joy, watching those adorable, little tow-haired boys squealing with pleasure playing together. But living in an apartment began to be a strain.

111

"Grace, if I continue to do so well, in a year my salary should increase to $1,500 a month," Steve announced to me one night. We dreamed about someday purchasing a home.

"That would be so great," I responded. I had discovered the joys of gardening and I thought it would be perfect to grow flowers and plants in an attractive yard.

During the first year of Mark's life, I was still able to substitute at La Canada High School, having located a competent childcare person. Chasing around two little active babies was exhausting, and they don't even have the courtesy of thanking you for cleaning the trail they leave behind them. To find better-mannered company, I read in a local newspaper about a group entitled Lawyers Wives of Los Angeles and I telephoned the membership chairperson. The woman's name is Ceil and she has been one of the sweetest and most efficient women I have ever known. Within months, I became extremely involved with this organization. Many social activities were planned to include our spouses. These industrious women became the nucleus of our social life.

Over the following five years, I held every board position available. Being so active afforded me the social outlet of evening meetings. This was an energy charged group and we were trained in a docent program to guide school age children on tours through the criminal courthouse in Los Angeles. In the courtroom, the students assumed the roles of prosecutor, defense, jury, and judge. What a great learning situation for the docents and the school children as well.

In the spring of 1971, Steve and I discovered that with his G.I. Bill, we would be able to purchase our first home in Pasadena. That G.I. bill allowed us to settle into a charming, little white house with a picket fence and a large backyard. For three years, we planted, painted, wallpapered, mowed lawns, and enjoyed all aspects of home ownership. We painted a sandbox yellow and played fire engine on the driveway. Mark's third birthday party was held at the fire station. Neighbors were friendly, and the boys and I walked around the block frequently to meet new people. The neighborhood people took care of each other and functioned like an extended family. Our lives were full and bursting with promise and fun.

Mark and I attended a parent education class at the local elementary school, and I learned so much about bonding with a child. Within a year, I enrolled the boys at Merryland Nursery School in Pasadena. For Brad, it was traumatic to give up to the headmistress, his beloved "blankie" three mornings a week. I now had some time to myself to run errands. Of course, there were always daily cares but there were no gray clouds to dim our bright future or our dreams.

Then a gentle nudge pushed me into further exploring what we might discover in the church as additional opportunities to expand our faith. One of my deepest blessings was attending La Canada Presbyterian Church. That was always part of the plan God used to grow my soul. The longing for God began as a quiet stirring. From this church, new women friends came into my life. We formed a small group and became sources of love, strength and consolation for each other.

Our weekly group meetings included sharing our struggles, reading inspiring Christian books, and praying for each other and our developing families. We stood together in our youthful, mothering days, assured that God was watching over us partially because the hand of a friend was always close and gentle. Casserole suppers were delivered when someone was ill or had an emergency or death in their family.

We stitched baby quilts for one another and knitted our lives together as well. Somehow, we learned to really bear each other's problems and share together our troubles with the confidence that God had sent angels to watch over our households. These Christian friends were great encouragers, so I began to teach Sunday school and participate in a weekly Bible class.

Seasons change and our days became increasingly more complicated. Those were amazing years that united and knotted us together. I see them as the times when life was kind and moderately serene and friends did things in a spirit of love sparked by a nudge they also felt. Faith had been the common denominator that sowed those seeds of love. Kindness ruled the hearts of the women in that small group. Through Susan Carey and Jan Roberts, I learned how patient love could be. These two friends persevered with me and taught me that friendship includes understanding not criticism. Jan became the nurturer role model I had so anticipated. Susan protects people and does so with dignity and confidentiality.

As we traveled down that busy road of life, we discovered the abundance of friendship and the promise that God was the gateway to peace and meaning. I learned it was a choice to follow that quiet inner voice. More and more, I began to recognize the hand of God in the small things in life. Meditating over scriptures felt like tapping into a silent and calming power. It seems to me now, that God had begun to prepare my soul for a deeper dedication to Him and His purpose for me. Invitations to learn more intrigued me. Sacred moments banished the gloomy days when parenting offered challenges and fatigue. Our small group prayed together for daily renewal.

Gradually, I learned to live in the promise that God would not only protect me but also sustain me in challenging moments. Kids got sick. Women suffered miscarriages. Over time, I began to trust God for a plan that would ensure a profound hope in the goodness of life. Deep in my heart, though, I knew myself to be a flawed person but was not yet wise enough to search out the help I would need. At times, raw anger was meted out towards my family in an unfair manner. God had a way of stirring up my comfortable nest. Eventually, I had to listen intently to my unevenness and brokenness during some very dark nights to keep from falling away from the light that I desired to be my guide.

There was little time to pause in our hurried life. Certain choices continued to enhance my life, especially the decision to move to La Canada. Mark was turning five years old and would be ready to begin kindergarten. Neither Steve nor I wanted him to be bussed to a school in Pasadena. Affluent people I knew considered it a wise decision to move to San Marino. That lovely community reminded me of my teenage years in Western Springs. Property values were climbing significantly, but our three offers to buy homes in San Marino were rejected. At an Easter picnic in Lacy Park, a good friend remembered that a house might be for sale in La Canada.

Steve and I, along with the boys, drove up to La Canada and peeked at the home. The house had some curb appeal, but it was a one-story ranch design that was not architecturally compatible with what we wanted. The couple selling their home explained that an offer had just been accepted. I rationalized that the house was not large enough anyway, were we to expand our family. But Steve immediately envisioned possibilities for the large back yard, which included a horse corral and some stately redwood trees.

A week later, the house fell out of escrow. Mr. and Mrs. Larsen accepted our full offer. From April until June, we packed boxes excitedly and took evening drives up to La Canada simply to drive past our new home. Our family doctor bought our modest home with the white picket fence on South Grand Oaks. Moving day arrived on June 28th, 1974. I remember that the listing broker left a six-pack of beer as a housewarming gift. McDonald's cheeseburgers would have been less tacky.

Opportunities awaited us. Whether our spirits have been strong or weak, I have always felt that this home where we raised our children was a prayer answered. A multitude of dreams have come true here. Through the prayers, I came to believe that God was working on our behalf. When our hearts were so full, we were blissfully unaware that our greatest tests of faith were yet to unfold.

XII

Jeremy's Younger Years

During the mid 1970's, the boys, Steve, and I discovered our days to be brimming over with activity. Many hours of the day were spent carpooling, driving in our red Oldsmobile to games, practices, schools, church, lessons, and parties. Yet, it seemed to me that someone was missing. There was a sense in me that a child needed to be born. A baby waited to be kicking in my womb.

I found myself, begging Steve. "Please, Steve, I want another baby."

"Well, I'm confident that we agreed on having two children," he replied fairly adamantly. "Two children are quite enough to care for," he insisted. This became the topic that we debated for months. Steve eventually acquiesced. I think he became worn down by my pressure or simply wondered who seemed to be missing. Who struggled to be birthed?

Soon after, we were pregnant. Those months raced by and I felt physically and emotionally strong and excited. I decorated the nursery in yellow and blue gingham. The local gynecologist, at a regularly scheduled appointment, recommended an actual calendar date for me to be induced. Our Lamaze instructor had previously advised against inducing a birth.

"Nature should take its course," she counseled us, listening to the heartbeat of our family member to be.

We discovered later that the real reason for a scheduled birth was for the doctor's convenience. He wanted to leave early for spring break because he had already planned his ski holiday.

The birthing day arrived. A bright, warm sun was rising outdoors. I could feel the life of this baby moving inside me. Inside my soul grew the sense of joy and anticipation. On the wall, the calendar displayed April Fools Day, April 1st, 1977. At 6:00 AM my friend Jan dropped by our house to send us off with a tiny bouquet of flowers, handpicked from her garden and tied with a Swiss ribbon. She is the kind of friend who will celebrate every occasion with extravagant joy.

Off we went, jubilant and proud to witness and participate in one last child's birth. Jeremy was born at Verdugo Hills Hospital in the early afternoon. Contractions convulsed my abdomen violently once the medication drip in the I.V. began. Something odd happened in the delivery room. I kept feeling as though I would faint and I normally gave birth easily.

"Grace, it's a little boy, and he is very small." Jeremy had not yet cried. The nurses whisked him away without giving me a chance to hold him on my stomach. I did not even know what he looked like. I wondered why I could not hold him. Steve appeared elated and left the hospital to tell the other children. That state of light-headedness kept returning to me, and I felt very woozy. Of course, I was expecting a pink fluff bundle to emerge. For the next couple hours, I kept drifting into another whirling world.

Dr. Baker, our pediatrician, and also a friend, came and woke me to inform me that Jeremy had been born prematurely and had developed aspiration pneumonia. His condition was serious and meant that he would be ambulanced to the neo-natal intensive care unit at Los Angeles Children's Hospital.

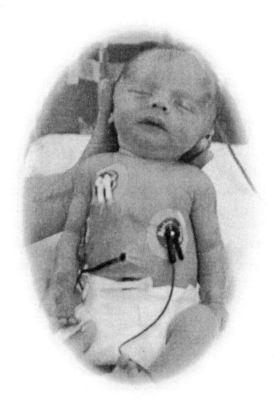

"Grace," Dr. Baker explained, "You need to get up and go and hold your baby and bond with him before he's transferred to Los Angeles." Weakened and stunned by this jolting news, I leaned against the doctor's arm and went to the nursery to visit our son. Jeremy looked so diminutive in the incubator, like a tiny chicken. *What had gone wrong?* I asked myself.

Through a connecting window, I could see my loyal friend Jan, who had stopped by for a "meet the baby" visit, but now, she seemed confused and dismayed. She attempted to use hand signals through the glass window.

"What will help?" she mouthed. Jan is so deep in my heart. All through that night, I prayed to God. In my questions, I became aware that we are all mortal human beings. When our pastor, Dr. Gary Demarest and his wife, Marily stopped by the hospital, I feared that something truly terrible had happened.

Gary told me, "We just came to pay a visit and see you and the baby."

In a very real sense, I was forced to let go of the outcome of Jeremy's well being. Clearly, this was not a "do it yourself" time. We leaned on many friends. People drove us to the hospital several times a day so I could use a breast pump. My mother flew out to help with our sons. Friends prepared meals. Jeremy's medical protocol required I.V.'s and Bilirubin lights for his jaundice and he was constantly connected to an oxygen tank.

On the third day, we were permitted to hold him for three minutes. Steve and I donned yellow paper masks and gowns. I recall feeling scared, exhausted and so relieved that friends were assuming so much responsibility for managing details at home. This was our first exercise in allowing friends to care for us in profound ways.

Jeremy came home two weeks later. His entire body fit in my hand. Not having developed a full sucking reflex, he required special attention. Teaching him how to nurse more rigorously was exhausting.

Weight dropped off my body quickly. Aside from needing to nurse every two hours, he soon began to thrive, and his peculiar, brown Mohawk haircut—shaved in ICU for the placement of electrodes—started to fill in.

Before very long, adorable Jeremy grew a full head of thick blond hair. Within several months, he had caught up physically to every other six-month-old baby.

Jeremy displayed curiosity about almost everything. Strapped into a bunting against my chest, he accompanied me everywhere. Along with Mark and Brad, we even went on a vacation that summer to Mammoth Lakes. Life and growth were happening in all of us.

Jeremy's sacrament of baptism took place on Christmas Day, 1977. Gary Demarest preached a sermon entitled *Too Good To Be True* and that was also the condition of my heart. A soloist sang a traditional song entitled "I Wonder As I Wander." This song became prophetic in his life. Both my parents and my brother Scott and his loving wife, Lynne were here for the holidays. Our neighbors and Steve's mother, Marie celebrated with us that happy Christmas. We planned a party to celebrate Steve's 40th birthday.

I glanced at the church bulletin and discovered this passage from the book of Isaiah, Chapter 25, to be the Old Testament Scripture lesson chosen for the Sunday of Jeremy's baptism.

> *The sovereign Lord will wipe away the tears from all faces; He will remove the disgrace of His people from all the earth. The Lord has spoken. In that day, they will say, "Surely this is our God; we trusted in Him, and He saved us. This is the Lord, we trusted in Him; let us rejoice and be glad in His salvation."*

Super abundance was the feeling I carried in my overflowing heart that Christmastide. How I loved this baby who had brought so much affirmation of life to us.

Before he became two years old, Jeremy mastered some wheel toys and preferred to play outdoors at Parent Education class at La Canada Presbyterian Church. This new program was an important outreach to the community and afforded lively and instructive information for parents. Some of those moms bonded with me to become lifelong friends.

One day, I wrote on my child observation sheet, "Jeremy is so physically active now that I can't keep up with him."

Annie Latta, the instructor commented, "Could it be that Mom is slowing down?"

Jeremy loved hats and kept changing them, an example of dramatic play. I was almost thirty-six years old and wearing many hats myself, attempting to teach part time and actively mother my children as well as stay involved in school and community activities.

Grandma Marie introduced Jeremy to the beloved world of dinosaurs that stimulated much imaginative play and she provided him an assortment of stuffed animals. From age two to eighteen, Jeremy either carried a tyrannosaurus or some kind of ball under his arm. He traipsed behind his older brothers, constantly annoying them with never ceasing questions about why things worked the way they do. We finally purchased a book called *How Things Work*. Through the window, I could glance at him watching Steve mow the lawn while asking him why he mowed the way he did. Jeremy was a solid companion and very observant.

Not too many children enjoy the joking around that happens when one's birthday is on April Fool's Day. Each year, the same eight playmates that had formed friendships at St. George's Nursery school came for a birthday party. Many of those festivities centered on a sports theme.

For a number of years, Jeremy played each June at Mrs. Pickering's piano recital. The first time Jeremy wore a navy blue blazer was to play Scott Joplin's *Maple Leaf Rag*. Once, he asked her if he could open the recital by playing the National Anthem, and he played it with great enthusiasm.

The La Canada Youth House Community Center had a T-Ball program, which instructed children how to play baseball. We were all cheering fans, and their awards certified everyone as a winner. I am not athletic at all, but I have always been attracted to sports programs that promote fun, fundamentals, and sportsmanship. Jeremy's competitive brothers would not have agreed with my philosophy, which is why they were all champion athletes. Jeremy enjoyed YMCA basketball, excelled at baseball, and was excited to be the goalie on the AYSO soccer team. Balls were appendages connected to his arms or legs.

In second grade, Jeremy wrote his first book. His first self-published work was entitled, *Hi, I'm Jeremy*. It shows Steve's positive impact on Jeremy:

> *I am very special for two reasons. I'm good at soccer and I am good at baseball. My home is very special to me. I like my home because I have a real cozy bed that is very warm.*
>
> *...My Dad takes me to school. My Dad takes me to school to ride my bike. My Dad makes hamburgers. My dad takes me to his office. My Dad is a good dad. My Dad is going to take just me to Catalina with our Indian Guides.*

Both of us encouraged our children to dream their own dreams. On the day of his eighth grade promotion, I wrote:

> *Remember, keep reaching for the stars. If you don't make the stars, you'll still land very close to the moon. We love you and are very proud of all your accomplishments. We think you are a great son and wish you the very best for your high school years.*

Jeremy's accomplishments in high school history qualified him to be recognized with a special plaque. Then quite suddenly in his junior year, he became disenchanted with life in La Canada. He began to disappear on wild adventures that we didn't understand.

Looking back, I do not believe he had any more insight than we did. Once, he ended up in Utah and Colorado, and Steve was dispatched to hunt for him and bring him back home. We had been living in an illusion of happiness.

Weren't we supposed to be happy if we had enough faith? I asked Steve and myself over and over again, as we struggled to find some baseline for balance.

His high school English teacher, a patient and kind woman, wrote:

> *I have known Jeremy only for about one semester, but have found him to be unfailingly polite and mature about accepting responsibility for his actions. He is concerned for others, and shows this by the way he treats me as well as his fellow students. Jeremy's intelligence and ability are unquestionable, but his performance has suffered in my class because of his unhappiness with La Canada and the whole ambiance here. Jeremy's lack of satisfaction with his life here at LCHS has evinced itself by his frequent unexcused absences and his failure to complete work. But, even in these negative circumstances, some of those positive character traits I mentioned come through. When Jeremy returned to my class after a protracted absence, he seemed most concerned that I would not take his truancies personally. I appreciated his concern for my feelings and his openness about sharing his frustrations with the school and the learning environment.*

I needed Jeremy to know that we were there for him and that he could confide in us. How worrisome it is to be out of contact with a child who you know could use your care and guidance. Once, when Jeremy was wandering about the world, I confronted him in a letter about my feelings:

Dear Jeremy,

Would you please try and understand what goes on in my heart when you always seem to be wandering? Where is the sensitive young man of four years ago who seemed so capable of expressing deep feelings for family members? I believed that there was some sort of unity between us—a promise that as members of a family, we had a sense of belonging to each other. And now it feels like you have pulled up stakes and split. I believe that there is an underlying assumption to life that promises and commitments are binding. It is costly to keep promises. When we break them, something is torn away from our character. That damages all the people who know and love you.

Of course, I forgive you, but I want you to remember that all human relationships are built on the foundations of promises exchanged and commitments made in sincere trust. When Dad and I desired to have children, we undertook an implicit commitment to provide a loving, safe, and nurturing environment in which you could grow up. Most people are tempted to flee from facing all the demons in their lives. Either we tend to go to the extreme of being totally absorbed in the pain or we flee or wander far away from the wound. It is a wound we want desperately to heal.

You, Jeremy, have a fascinating story to share. Despite serious challenges at birth, you survived, became resilient and overcame difficulties. This is your character. You were a charming and delightful child. On the quest and journey to discover your own identity, at one point God sent you people with whom you shared your struggles and they helped lead you closer to the true source of love…God. Don't clutch on to the old pattern of running away. That never works. Our problems and our emotional baggage accompany us to every new destination.

What you can trust is the inner voice that shows a better way; you know that voice and you used to turn to it often. Maybe you feel nothing but loneliness and emptiness but keep repeating, "God loves me and God's love is really enough." Remember this place called home in La Canada. It will always be a place where you can hang your hat and your heart and dump your stuff.

Love,
Mom

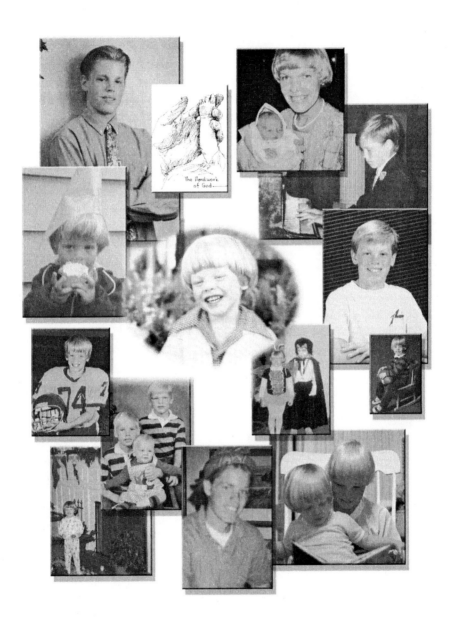

XIII

RETROSPECT AND PROSPECT:
BRAD'S JOURNEY

SCRAWLED ACROSS THE FRONT PAGE of a now faded, church bulletin in my scratchy handwriting is a recipe that my mother used to bake frequently. It was her distinctive recipe for French Silk chocolate pie. That ivory colored bulletin is dated January 3, 1971. My parents were visiting our Pasadena apartment over the Christmas holidays. So it was a natural choice to select that first Sunday of the New Year as the day for second son Bradley Walter Galton's baptism.

"Don't forget to beat, on high, for five minutes after you add each of the four eggs," my mother instructed me. Just why we were whispering in church, I don't remember. Food preparation and going to the market took up much of my time and weekly allowance during their visits.

"I suppose it helped to rationalize their plane fare," I mentioned to my brother, Scott, who hosted them graciously whenever they traveled to Philadelphia.

Brad was three months old on that day and had been an extremely, content baby, rarely crying or demanding.

Most of the day, he sat in his infant seat, smiling and gurgling, watching Mark play. Whereas Mark constantly sought relentless activity and attention, Brad came into this world a mellow baby, observant of the action around him, but seldom fussy. For hours, he was able to sit in his wooden, expandable playpen simply noticing everything around him. He seemed so satisfied. Much of the Christmas holiday he was perched in his infant seat under the decorated Christmas tree, fascinated by the bright colored lights. He wore a red cotton Santa Claus romper complete with cap.

My mother was always partial to him. I think she appreciated his alertness to his surroundings. As a little boy, he would race across the room and trustingly leap into the air in order to be scooped up into her arms. Brad was an affectionate child and derived his middle name, Walter, from my father.

Dr. Gary Demarest, senior pastor of the Presbyterian Church, preached the sermon that day entitled *Retrospect and Prospect*. Thirty-five years later, that sermon title seems fitting as a metaphor to describe Brad's journey through life. In contemplating that childhood stage of his life, I ponder the qualities that made him such a unique child.

Brad is a fine, concise, to the point, and almost terse writer. Rummaging through his school mementos, I found a report entitled *The Dogfish Shark*. He had drawn a comprehensive number of pictures of this classification of sharks depicting their digestive, nervous, reproductive, circulatory, and skeletal systems. The report was instructive to even an adult. Each chapter contained the captions, "What I did" and "What I observed."

His teacher commented, "You have done a fine job. You have good information which you have presented in an organized and logical manner." Brad has always been able to analyze and reflect on what he reads and writes.

This aptitude for writing put him in honors English classes.

Miss Ober summarized his first grade experience:

> *Brad is dependable and a hard worker. He is making fine progress and takes an active part in all classroom activities. Initiative and study habits are excellent.*

Parents in La Canada worry excessively about their children's progress and parent-child conferences cause some anxiety for parents who so desire to have their offspring excel. The praise he received was well deserved. With Brad, we were always assured that his teachers would be more than satisfied. Early in his development, I noticed that he wrote well and creatively. As a small boy, he became animated on weekly visits to the library. His eagerness to learn new information astounded me.

School districts in California were authorized to provide special educational opportunities to students, who after consideration of all pertinent data, evidenced exceptional intellectual and scholastic ability. State test scores identified Brad as a mentally gifted minor, and he became eligible to receive qualitatively different opportunities for learning. The purpose of the gifted program was to provide challenging and rewarding programs for talented students. The plan involved a student being pulled out of regular class 200 minutes per week per semester. Brad thrived in this stimulating environment and became a conscientious student throughout most of high school until other social distractions absorbed his attention.

Brad was invited to participate in Academic Decathlon during his junior year of high school. Being a team member was a grueling test in mental keenness. Mental acuity was demanded in ten academic areas including economics, fine arts, language, literature, mathematics, science, social studies, essay writing, and debate. Mr. James McDonnell taught these mental athletes and the students competed in stiff competitions against 70 other high schools in Southern California. It is not an easy process to win a decathlon gold medal. In addition to brainpower, intellectual endurance is a key requirement for success. Our family took pleasure in watching Brad participate.

Saturdays were competition days and frequently conflicted with other sports events in which Brad was engaged. Brad managed his time well. One event in the decathlon was called *Super Quiz*. That year's five-question subject was about the history of flight. Brad has always been capable of storing a vast amount of information in his mind and then recalling it when that information needs to be retrieved. Although stressful for him, Brad did very well in all these competitions.

Brad's principle challenge in the competition was learning how to manage the anxiety caused by rigorous championships. He revealed some apprehension before important events. Family members could sense this tension. On certain occasions, prior to swim meets, I could observe his shoulders shaking.

Since almost the beginning of his high school experience, Brad displayed enthusiasm about attending one of the University of California campuses. Our objective as parents was to encourage our children to apply to the most competitive school of their choice. Part of our agreement included paying for college but not graduate school. Brad chose to attend a large university, which was affordable but also included a party scene lifestyle at the beach.

During a difficult period at the University of California at Santa Barbara, Brad thought hard about his future goals and objectives. That environment provided too many distractions and Brad lost vision for a period of time. Later he wrote about those times in a letter to Steve and me:

A long-term career prospect is invaluable in keeping a good perspective to my educational purpose. This is what will plant my feet to the ground so that I can get a clear focus. Fortunately, I know that I am already leaning towards a legal profession. This affords me the strategic advantage of time. I can be thinking ahead into what areas of law I may venture while making contacts and inquiries accordingly. I want to absorb as much knowledge of the subject as possible. In this way, I should be able to stay competitive in my field and score well on the Law School Admission Test. Before I can start any of this, however, I need to mature into a competent decision maker. Priority setting is one of the most important factors in living a normal life, let alone having a successful college record. To do this, I must first find out what my priorities are. Right now, concentrating on rebuilding my study skills is of the utmost importance. No matter how it gets done, even if I need help from outside sources, studying must take my undivided attention. After that, things will begin to fall into place because I will have built confidence and self-reliance.

Brad decided against entering the legal profession. I really don't know all the factors he considered in arriving at that decision. Increasingly, Brad showed interest in finance and business. He frequently discusses with us the criteria he adopts for setting priorities.

Brad eventually obtained his Bachelor of Arts degree from UCSB and entered a financial career. For three years he studied earnestly and with some intensity to pass the requirements to become a certified financial analyst. That was a high hurdle to pass over and demanded great self-discipline.

Music has been another life-long pursuit and his interest began with eight years of piano study. Brad learned how to relax by teaching himself how to play the guitar. Break Dancing became a popular activity in the eighth grade and Brad and his buddies put on quite a performance in a talent show. In our church, Brad sang in a few musicals. He is interested in various styles of music and enjoys attending rock concerts.

Athletics filled his childhood spare time. His family and friends were proud and gratified with his many accomplishments. That concentration and ability to focus were key ingredients for his success on the playing fields. In the box I preserve, which contains important mementos, I discovered dozens of awards for presidential fitness, swimming medals, water polo ribbons accompanied by newspaper clippings, and baseball trophies. "Come on, Brad, you can hit another home run." was a cheer frequently screamed from his fans sitting in the bleachers.

Playing Gladiator football distinguished Brad from his brothers who never played football. Under the achievements certificates, I found a letter written to Brad from his coach when Brad was in junior high school:

Dear Brad,

    The purpose of this letter is to thank you for the 100% effort you put out this fall on behalf of the Pee Wee football program. I was especially pleased by your willingness to take on the learning of the third position in record time to avoid a team catastrophe of having no playable fullback and also your emergency crash course on offensive signal calling. You are one of the players who has learned some of the lessons that a sport like football can teach: self-sacrifice, self-discipline, and the willingness to subjugate your personal glory for the good of the team. Congratulations, Brad, on a great learning year.

    Coach Daniel Lewis

As he would explain to his dying brother Mark, Brad has ventured into territory with "diverse emotional landscapes." I think he felt a jealousy and sibling rivalry toward his brother to compete and win the same awards in life. In a letter to Mark, he wrote:

    I have failed to see that I have a race of my own. And though many times I have enjoyed basking in the brilliance of your light, I have also been blinded by it. Sometimes that has made it difficult for me to find my own path and the truth that I am valuable in other, perhaps more subtle, ways. There is beauty in all the different places within a family, but I stopped embracing my role because it didn't get the same type of recognition.

I see some wisdom in his observation and realize that as an avid hiker, Brad has peered at the peaks and valleys in life through a different lens than I have ever used.

Being near the precipice of any edge frightens me. I'm too afraid of going over the edge. Brad is bold and less fearful.

Brad is amazingly courageous to dauntlessly face himself. Though he has endured family struggles, job changes and personal challenges, I am confident that he will continue to see the abundant resources with which he has been gifted and envision a confident path ahead of him.

Dear Son Brad,

Though your path may seem difficult, you need not be afraid. You already know the Guide who has promised us His invisible presence. Do not fear anymore. Keep observing everything on the rough road as well as the paved highway. Have no regrets in leaving behind what is too burdensome. You are finding great freedom. No one is exempt from difficulties and pain. You have climbed numerous mountains and the burden has been heavy to carry at times alone. Keep moving forward and signs of new life will emerge. We all belong on this path of discovering who God intends for us to be. Your foothold will be secure. Celebrate in retrospect and anticipate the prospects of fulfilling your dreams. May the purpose of your life be accomplished. I am proud to be your mother.

Love,
Mom

XIV

THE LANGUAGE OF PINK TINTED GLASSES:
LOOKING AT LISSY

THE ROSEBUD on the communion table joyfully announces the birth of Elisabeth Grace Galton, born on May 24th, 1979.

The words jumped out from the page on the church bulletin. I turned to gaze at my husband sitting next to me in the pew, and I fully comprehended the blessing. He placed his arm around my shoulder. Everyone was finally present in our family circle. An enormous sense of contentment and pride filled my whole being. Was there any logical explanation that Lissy would debut at Huntington Memorial Hospital weighing in at 6 pounds ½ ounce and stretching a full nineteen inches?

After a miscarriage the year before, I gave up hope that there would ever be a female in our home. Steve insisted firmly that this was absolutely the last unknown person that I should ever consider missing in our family. I sustained a difficult, almost perilous pregnancy. When the gynecologist suggested that the pregnancy might not be viable and I should consider other options, I phoned a psychologist whom I trusted.

"Grace, follow your heart in this dilemma, pray and then leave the matter in God's hands," he advised. God and I talked about this quandary daily. How ridiculous was my negotiating a deal with God, the creator of life.

"God, if this pregnancy works out okay, I will be the best mother ever," I swore my oath.

My parents were visiting for the birth and impatient that their return airfare might increase if I had predicted the due date inaccurately. After a doctor's visit, when he suggested that we might be another week waiting, I entered the bathroom door, locked it and sat down on the floor to accomplish twenty sit-ups.

"Why, dear God, do I behave so stupidly when my folks are here? And why do I even care about their convenience?" But I did. In the morning, there were sufficient readiness signs to warrant going to the hospital. The trip in the car was somewhat tense. For nine months, I worried constantly that there might be a problem with the pregnancy but acted willfully against the doctor's advice to terminate the actual pregnancy. I remember telephoning Nancy en route to warn her that I felt fearful and wondered how I would cope with a fourth son, especially if he had problems.

Steve and I checked in at the hospital and spent the entire afternoon playing gin rummy. Although I had decided against any medication for the hard contractions, I regretted that decision. In those days, we prided ourselves on a completely natural childbirth. Soon I was wheeled into the delivery room with Steve beside me solicitous and caring. At 8:10 PM, there were two long pushes and out came Lissy. Steve and I were looking for the body parts that should have belonged to Jonathan, the baby boy I expected. Instead here she was squealing and finally on my breast. Mary Ellen, my childhood doll, would have been so proud of this beautiful baby girl. Lissy yawned, arched her back, crossed her arms behind her head and went back to sleep. I screamed with pure joy and Steve took her in his strong arms to gaze upon her beauty. Thirty-seven years passed before I held either a baby sister or a baby daughter. Dr. Puttler rushed out of the delivery room to phone his wife. This was big news.

Nothing is pasted into Lissy's baby book except her name. Her Tupperware box, under my bed is crammed with mementos and they fill in all the details of her life nicely. Lisanna was my idea for a name. Steve thought that sounded like an Italian dinner. Gwyneth didn't seem quite right either. Finally, Steve agreed to the name Lissy, if on her passport it read Elisabeth Grace. Neither on her schoolwork or her career resumes, has she used any name except Lissy, but she has vociferously warned me that she plans to break the chain of the Grace name.

"No child belonging to me will carry on the tradition of this name." Lissy is fearless in expressing strong opinions.

Why do I so adore this young woman? Love poured out from our first encounter when I touched her delicate toes and dimples. Lissy appeared quite shy as a tiny child, but now I attribute her former reticence as primarily a family dynamic.

Older brothers usually dominated the dinner conversation discussing their sports and school activities. She was just less demanding than the rest of us for air time.

Her pre-school teacher, Miss Pam, had already tuned into Lissy's special interests and skills. Miss Pam wrote:

Lissy seems to enjoy all facets of her pre-school experience. She eagerly participates in all table activities, enjoying a small muscle task like cutting as much as a tactile experience with finger painting. New items, such as eyedropper painting offer a challenge to her and it is not uncommon for her to totally involve herself in the process for a long period of time. She moves as her interests dictate, preferring little direction from adults. Lissy also enjoys the opportunity to socialize with her friends. Yard time offers this chance for vigorous social situations and involved dramatic play.

I was delighted to mother such a dainty child—even after hours of pre-school, her clothes remained immaculately clean. Years later, her teacher, Miss Carol, admitted that the minute Lissy arrived in the classroom, they changed her out of her pinafore into some grubby play clothes and then changed her back into her smocked dresses before my return.

Lissy accompanied me everywhere except once. Steve, Grandma Marie, Mark, Brad, and I went to Europe for a two-week trip. Separation anxiety affected me terribly. Upon return home, the babysitter announced that Lissy and Jeremy had acted normally except that Lissy had watched the movie *Annie* twice each day. I suspect Lissy felt orphaned those two weeks.

Our family would attend the Rose Parade every year, and one of Lissy's childhood dreams was to be a Rose Princess. By the age of nine, she had perfected the royal Rose Princess wave of "elbow, elbow, wrist, wrist, wrist." In her senior of high school, she was honored to receive letters informing her that she was being considered for the Rose Court. Once dismissed from the running, she used the compliment and disappointment as cause to further involve herself in both church leadership responsibility and community service. Her father had sent a card with flowers, saying, "You will always be my rose queen."

Lissy loved tap dancing, tumbling, ballet, and all forms of dance. She always remembered special occasions with cards that she had designed. On her elementary school report cards, the teachers marked work habits and citizenship with a plus, indicating an area of superior strength. Another hobby was writing. At age eleven, she kept a journal of her first, month long trip to Europe. Frequently, she wrote poems about her love for Michigan where we owned a summer cottage and returned each season.

One of Lissy's strongest attributes is her attentiveness to celebrating special occasions, especially her messages written on birthday and anniversary cards. As a child, she attached personalized artwork to her notes and greeting cards. Steve and I were astounded to realize her amazing ability to express tender and sensitive feelings.

When Lissy was thirteen, she wrote an essay that I discovered only recently, and I began to wonder if she had felt pressure growing up. The title is *My Mother Expects So Much of Me*. Before the tension of high school and the time when girls want to separate from their moms, she wrote this passage:

My mother has always been my role model in life. She is clever, creative, sensitive, caring and smart. My mother has always been a very intelligent person. She believes that I should live up to her. I try to in every way. It is very hard. Here are some particular things she compares me on:

The first and most important is grades. If I don't get a three point five, at least I'll be grounded for a month. Math was never a good subject for her, and so she doesn't think that I'll do well in that. She does think that I should get A's in everything else.

Secondly, I do many after school activities. They take up lots of time. My PE teacher would like to put me on a track team. He talked to the coach at La Crescenta Valley High School, and they run three miles a day. My parents thought this was a great idea because I am the fastest girl runner in my class. I think this is a good thing for me to do, but I wish they would let me decide on this.

I have also taken piano lessons for seven years, and practicing forty-five minutes a day was not my idea. Hip Hop class, Jazz dance, babysitting, National Charity League are other activities I'm involved in. These require time and commitment, and I can do only my best.

My mother was also class president. This year, she asked me why I didn't run for office. I told her that I had been secretary and had been on the school council, and school patrol other years. I believe that my mother is really proud of me even though she wishes I were more of this, and less of that. Trying my hardest to be someone that she can admire means everything to me.

Wanting Lissy to be proud of me seems equally significant as the years go by. Steve and I were especially proud of her performance in her final piano recital, which came after twelve long years of dedicated study. Excellence and dedication describe Lissy. During her four years at LCHS, she was an editor of the school newspaper, and she has received awards in both Math and English.

Thanks to her cherished tutor, Laurie, Lissy was recognized for her performance on the Golden State exam in math. She was a member of Chorus, Peer Counseling, and Students Against Drunk Drivers.

Lissy expanded her worldview by traveling and living abroad. Through the American Field Service program, she lived in southern France, serving at a day care center while living on a dairy farm with a French family in a rural village. She was a youth leader in her church, and she has volunteered on numerous service projects in Mexico.

As Lissy learned through volunteer work, she was also giving back to the community. She was an aide to Governor Pete Wilson in the Youth In Government Program her junior year, where she learned a dedication to the values of a working democracy. In the San Marino Chapter of National Charity League she worked as a childcare center volunteer at Huntington Hospital. She has also worked with seniors at The Scripps Home, volunteered at The Pasadena Humane Society, and helped children at Los Angeles County Hospital.

Steve and I somehow missed the deadline for putting a graduation message to Lissy in her High School yearbook. So instead, we ran a special note to her in the newspaper:

> *Dear Lissy,*
>
> *You are our beloved daughter. In you, we see goodness, beauty, and love. Be patient with yourself in life. Keep walking straight following the path to God. Reach for your dreams and hopes. Continue to think through your choices wisely. Own your mistakes. Be a faithful friend. Trust the depth of God's presence in you. Carry our love in your heart always.*
>
> *Love,*
> *Mom and Dad*
>
> *P.S.—We did not find you in a cabbage patch.*

Regrets like these line the drawers of everyone's yesteryears, and I have my share of skeletons in the closet. One of these skeletons is a cat.

Lissy wanted a kitten, but I am not too fond of animals. She had already outgrown her dolls and dollhouses when we selected a cat from a pet store in Pasadena. Her attention was now devoted to "Kitty," a white Persian with blue eyes who slept on Lissy's pillow every night. My friend, Pauline, called Kitty "D.C."—an abbreviation for Designer Cat—because of her blue eyes and fair coloring; she looked like a Galton. I believe Lissy whispered her secrets into Kitty's ear much the same way I did to my doll, Mary Ellen.

Kitty shed a lot of fur, and her litter box smelled terribly. So the week of Lissy's college graduation—after four years of my personal attention lavished on this animal—I threatened Lissy to move her Kitty to Portland with her, or I would take the cat to the pound. Lissy was horrified.

While we were up in Portland celebrating Lissy's college graduation, Kitty somehow got out of the house. For months, I drove up and down the streets of La Canada searching and calling out, "Kitty. Kitty Kitteeee…" All of God's creatures need food, and coyotes are no exception. This is the comfort I narrowly cling to.

Lissy has been a strong female presence that I need in my life. She has always seen the world in a relentlessly positive way. Though life's journey may not always be roses, and its winters may test the soul, her soft resiliency makes it seem like perpetual spring.

XV

THE LANGUAGE OF COUNSELING: FULLER SEMINARY

I WISH I HAD A PENNY for every hour I have spent in the aisles of grocery stores. Would I ever be wealthy! Our pantry at home always needed to be replenished. Initially, I thought taking classes at seminary would be similar. Going to seminary hardly resembles going to the grocery story, I soon ascertained. That was the first lesson I learned. You do not pick up a few items that you think you might need for your pantry or for your dinner.

Within Fuller Seminary, there are three distinct schools: the School of Theology, the School of World Missions, and the School of Psychology. Each school has a demanding curriculum and a degree program. Certainly, there was a wealth of sustenance on which to feast. Glancing through the curriculum catalog was like reviewing a menu in a gourmet restaurant. I wanted a taste of all the appetizers. I never intentionally decided to attend graduate school to study theology. That responsibility, I thought, belonged in the domain of pastors. In my spiritual situation, I had been asking Jesus to be my friend and teacher since I was three years old. Sometimes, however, serious seekers need to be set free to discover for themselves what it means to be a person created in the image of God. Already, I had a rudimentary theological knowledge, gleaned from those compulsory college chapels at Wheaton College when the boys weren't distracting me. My appetite and thirst for the tangible presence of God in my daily life led me now to explore more fully what it would mean to be a serious follower of Christ. My theology is more deeply etched in my heart than stated in a formal creed or doctrine. Symbols of my deepening faith are found among my valuable spiritual collectibles. For example, on my bedroom bureau is a paperweight with a worn piece of brown felt, glued to the bottom. Typed on a piece of faded peach colored paper under the glass top is a two-year-old picture of me with a typed poem:

Only one life,
Twill soon be past.
Only what's done
for Christ will last.

In addition to the paperweight is my plastic Jesus night light which glows in the dark, my perfect attendance Sunday School pin and my mother's gold cross. These symbols of my faith were the seeds planted in my life long ago along with all those hundreds of Bible verses which I memorized in competition with my brother, Bob.

When I finally did get to Lake Ripley Summer Camp in Wisconsin, I attended an outdoor bon fire service on the last evening. In the long ago tradition of this camp, this last night service was referred to as a "Faggot Service." As was the innocence of the times, the term *faggot* simply meant "a bundle of small sticks." Campers went out into the woods to collect them. I don't remember if my brother, Bob, came with me. He may have been making a lanyard or getting a head start on memorizing the next year's verses. Each child who wanted to shine as Christ's light in the world lit a match to their faggot and placed it on the bon fire before describing their conversion or transforming experience that week.

I was now eight years old and still affected by my baptism in the fount at Lorimer Memorial Baptist Church in front of the crimson velvet curtain. When I got dunked, gasping in the blessed water, I expected that something dramatic would happen. I tried to loiter in the fount, waiting for my telegram from God. But I became cold and soaking wet, and my white baptismal robe was plastered to my skin. Dr. I.C. Peterson held a handkerchief over my nose and I prayed that God would send me as a missionary to Africa. That was my conversion story I told to the campers and leaders in front of the bonfire as my sticks burned.

I could have continued my story with any one of the dozens of conversion experiences I've had—Baptists are always being saved, over and over again. I shared the one where I ran down the aisle, at age seven, to receive a new heart in Jesus. A child evangelist spoke of black hearts being cleansed by the blood of Jesus. I responded to the altar call after he sawed a lady in half —presumably his wife—during a magic show at Lorimer Memorial Baptist Church. There wasn't enough time though, to describe more than one "being saved" event because the other "sunbeams for Jesus" were waiting to relate their stories.

Meeting Steve, teaching French, and raising a large family took me away from that missionary track, but I know God kept inviting me to deeper places spiritually. My friends helped me maintain a keen interest in church activities and I was faithful in service. Fortunately, I was involved in many capacities and kept on meeting incredible Christians. In some ways, I already was acutely aware that I had participated in the power of the Spirit and was being called into a deeper expression of living out my faith.

Enough of life's challenges had already humbled me by the time I was thirty-five and now I was turning forty-eight years old. Occasionally, I disappointed my family and myself. One of my struggles was dealing with the way I acted out my anger. Already, I had discovered numerous challenges in marriage, parenting, and teaching. Some of those paths were steep and rocky. I now wish my brother, Scott, had lived closer to counsel me. I trust him with all my being as an advisor.

My anger problems and resentments forced me into some sobering and serious years in therapy. I was concerned about the effect it had on my marriage.

Steve was fairly clear on the matter. "Grace, if you don't find some help for your verbal abusiveness, we're not going to last together."

I knew how deeply I had been influenced by my own family of origin and had tried to flee to California to pretend that the damage hadn't happened. What I discovered in a therapeutic environment unlocked mysteries related to family patterns and the roles of family members and unspoken rules that unconsciously dictate our family dynamics in the next generation. How depressing it was to own the possibility that I had passed damaging behaviors to my children.

When I was thirteen years old, I made a vow to "never do it like my parents." What was I still needing, and how could I get free of the past? I had never been liberated from the rage at the perceived injustices in my past. Sputtering flames of anger got released, and with my therapist, we gently looked at the smoldering coals and embers symbolizing the unresolved issues. How liberating it was to have my thoughts and feelings welcomed and challenged in a protected and safe therapeutic environment. From learning how to express the emptiness, I received healing and became interested in unlocking the fragility of others' pain and loneliness.

In the winter of 1988, I was praying more than ever before. Four years earlier at a church family camp, I had experienced a sensation that felt spiritual that I could scarcely explain to anyone. When I prayed, that past feeling and stillness often restored me. A trusted friend, Karen Berns, then a pastor at LCPC, was in a small group with me. Despite her rigorous schedule and all the demands on her time, she set aside an hour each week to meet, talk, and pray. Together, we listened for God in the quietness of our solitude.

That autumn, our second son, Brad, left for college and I hung up my teaching hat. Just for fun, I decided to audit an Ethics class at Fuller Seminary, a few miles from our home. Teaching the class with great warmth and wit was Dr. Lewis Smedes, then on the ethics committee at Huntington Hospital. Young people looking twenty-five years old dominated the class. Our project was studying case studies and debating the wisdom of making life and death choices. Many of the students reflected the attitudes of persons lacking in much life experience. Frequently, I vociferously disagreed with some of their decisions. During that semester, I began to take some pride in being my truest self. I spoke out fearlessly, justifying certain decisions based on what I had learned in life. Dr. Smedes continued to call on me. Often, my position was unpopular. Twice, we shared a conversation over coffee. On those occasions, we discovered our Michigan roots. Lewis Smedes and Dr. Ray A. Anderson encouraged me to become a counselor and wrote my recommendations to the School of Psychology at Fuller Seminary.

Lewis Smedes was a mentor and a modest man. His example of humility inspired me. In a note, after missing my Fuller Graduation party in June 1993, he wrote:

Could you possibly forgive me? Excuse me? Tolerate me? Suffer me? I am unworried about your evening. It was, I am sure a fantastic celebration. Add to it one tardy, but no less hearty congratulations. You are a pride to us. And you are a very special joy to me.

Warmly,
Lew

Initially, I wondered if God had sent me to Fuller so that I could experience being in over my head. My insecurity made me undertake the academic challenge too strictly. I got up nearly every morning at 4:00 AM to study. Within a year, I learned that the program gently moved us classmates into deeper ways of living and thinking that challenged our preconceived ideas of being therapists.

Once accepted into the competitive Marriage and Family program, our class of forty studied Psychology from a family systems perspective. Various counseling theories, adolescent and child development, alcoholism and other addictions, pharmacology, diagnostic tools, feminine issues, crisis management, marital therapy, family therapy, and ethnicities were some of the curriculum we pursued. Behind a screen, we practiced doing therapy and writing verbatim exchanges as well as analyzing our progress. The hardest course for me was Statistics.

An additional requirement was serving as a trainee in an approved site for two years. Mike, my supervisor, evaluated my work weekly. Mike helped me so much in integrating theory with clinical practice. Part of the uniqueness of the Fuller program was the requirement of studying theology and developing a model for integrating psychology and theology. We learned to think of true spiritual conversion as a deep change in the inner woman or man based on what Christ has already done for us.

That belief has helped me view people from God's perspective as wounded individuals needing insight and love. We may be created in the image of God, but most of us, I believe, are fallen and wounded image bearers.

Attending Fuller Seminary was one of the highlights of my life. It did not become clear to me until my second year that when I went there, I had truly been "called" by God to obtain the credentials helpful in developing a pastoral care ministry in my own church called *The Stephen Ministry*, named after St. Stephen, the first martyr of the Christian Church.

The plush throw blanket presented to me at the end of ten years of Stephen Ministry service—and everything that I learned—is a treasured personal collectible. I place this blanket over my knees in the morning when I pray: it warms my spirit and blesses the decision to channel God's unconditional love into the worn down pilgrims who trudge across my path.

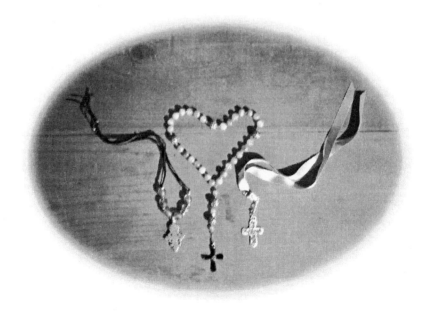

XVI

LISSY AND HER BROTHERS

BY OCTOBER in Lissy's senior year at LCHS, she decided to forego the craziness of the senior crush. The others panicked, searching for the perfect school to complement their perfect SAT scores and their perfect grade point averages. Some had even raised their GPA's to 4.3 by taking advanced placement courses. Not Lissy. According to her, this folderol seemed unnecessary. Our daughter has a definite inclination to decrease the pressure of stress.

An early decision application for admission meant filling out just one application for one college. Lissy's choice was Willamette University, a top tier school and the oldest university west of the Mississippi River. Willamette is across from the state capitol building in Salem, Oregon. The campus sprawls out through manicured quad areas over beautiful lawns with turn-of-the-century red brick buildings. A stream meanders through the main quad, Canadian geese swim in the chilly water, and every spring the barren stick trees blossom with beautiful pink flowers.

We dropped her off for her freshman year, and she stood out in the street, waving and waving good-bye. With a broad smile on her face, she was reassuring me she would be happy. There was a bittersweet quality in my waving, and I cried in the car, remembering how I forced her to finish piano study.

In a Mother's Day gift book, Lissy wrote on the inside page:

May 11, 1997

Dear Mom,
In two weeks, I'll turn eighteen, and soon, I'll be leaving for college. It seems like yesterday that I was leaving for kindergarten. I remember how hard it was to leave you, and venture off on my own. But your reassurance and support let me go and enjoy it. And I know when you let go of me once again, your continuous support will enable me to go off and have fun again. Thank you for all the years of love and care you have given to me. I'm going to miss you terribly when I leave, but you will always be close to my heart.

I love you,
Lissy

Lissy did make a smooth transition to college life and avoided rough and stormy adjustments. She realized her potential and enjoyed what the university had to offer academically and socially. On the telephone, I listened to long running sagas about life in the sorority house.

Christmas 1997, her freshman year, was a bustling time. After a six-year Ticktocker program in the National Charity League, the December debutantes would be recognized for their community service. Lissy had accumulated over 700 hours of service. San Marino National Charity League provided an enchanted evening in the ballroom at the Beverly Regent Hotel in Beverly Hills. We smiled at our gorgeous daughter, on the arm of her father, as she made her official St. James bow to society.

Four years after arriving at Williamette, right on cue, she strutted out on the stage in her high-heeled shoes to receive her Bachelor of Arts degree in English. Misty-eyed, I watched the baby of the family finish college. Prone to understatement, Lissy is an incredibly accomplished woman. She is poised and capable of meeting every challenge.

Some of her maturity and resourcefulness may have come from the time she was somewhat stranded in Seville, Spain. She was on her way there for a cross-cultural study semester when all of her luggage was stolen at the train station. With only enough money to buy six outfits to last three months, she learned her version of "roughing it."

Columbia Sportswear, one of the largest quality sellers of skiwear, offered Lissy a job after graduation as a

Materials Research Assistant. She managed the fabric library for the sportswear and outerwear departments. Lissy enjoyed her first post-college career position and lived on a beautiful tree-lined avenue in downtown Portland.

A year after her brother Mark died, Lissy accepted a position at an advertising agency near Manhattan Beach to be closer to her family. Her personality suits her career as a strategic planner at a company named Team One.

Lissy realizes the importance of family life and spends time supporting us. Several years ago, in a school essay, she described the impact Brad had made on her life:

> *Brad used to tell me I was adopted, and not really part of the family. But no brother could love his sister as much as he loved me. That's why there has been no greater influence in my life than my brother Brad. After surviving constant torment and teasing from him the first ten years of my life, I finally realized how special he is and just how much his relationship means to me.*
>
> *His effect on my life began with childhood memories and has developed into a strong friendship that has never ceased to grow. As an older brother, Brad felt the necessity to bully, and also befriend me from the very beginning of our relationship. I can remember as a little girl my parents leaving to go out, and entrusting my care to Brad as a babysitter. Usually, this was not a good idea because people's perceptions of babysitting can vary quite a bit. Brad felt this was the appropriate time to invite 150 or so of his closest friends over for a get together. This would usually leave me cleaning up peoples' messes, fixing snacks and getting blamed for the whole thing. Now as I look back with admiration for these parties, I can't help but laugh at all the crazy things we did. Sometimes, I wish I had the same boldness to pull off the pranks he did.*
>
> *Another babysitting incident was when he thought it would be funny, to lock me out of the house just for a little scare. I decided it would be funnier, if I ran and hid in the back yard for at least*

an hour. I think it was the first time I had seen him so vulnerable. Maybe Brad was a little scared. He had never looked so sad, and I had never heard his voice filled with so much emotion.

Besides the babysitting catastrophes, I have so many other memories I cherish of the fun we had as kids. I remember the picnics we had in our tree house, and how my other brothers would eat my hot dogs that we cooked for dinner. So Brad would split his hot dog in half, or steal mine right back saying, "Lis, I'm here for you today, tomorrow, and every day after."

Brad demonstrated the necessity of the need for us siblings to love each other, and he was always the first to offer me a hug or to stand by me in a tough time. He was also the first of four children to play the piano, and, after continuously listening to him practice, I decided some day, I would be just as good. I'm now starting my twelfth year playing. I'm indebted to Brad for inspiring me to take up such a magnificent instrument. But it's natural for him to bring happiness and joy in my life, because he has been doing it for so long, and I think its what Brad is best at.

Now as older kids, he has become a treasured friend and confidant. Brad never fails to call me once a day. Brad's friendship is irreplaceable. When he calls me, he is always a hundred percent caring, understanding and a great listener. It is amazing to be completely honest with someone and know he is always going to love me anyway.

Lissy describes the shock and terror of her brother, Jeremy, being lost in the mountains and her flying home and waiting paralyzed with fear:

Hourly check-ins offered no new information, only that the search parties had to go home because bad weather was settling in. With each passing hour, my anxiety rose. The only thing I was capable of was spontaneous bouts of hysteria. We turned-on the news only to see that Southern California was having the worst

161

storm in years and that the mountains were being dumped with snow. So, we changed the channel, and saw a story about a Portland man whose body had been found after he was lost in the woods. These were moments when I thought I was either in Hell, or unable to wake up from a nightmare. But it was all too real. And my thoughts became darker and colder with the night.

When my parents called with my flight information, my mind was made up. I won't forget what it felt like to give up. In some ways it was easier to lose hope because I wasn't setting myself up to be devastated again. But now I feel like I let Jeremy down giving up on him so soon. Mostly though, I feel like I let myself down. The agony of deciding what to pack for his funeral was accompanied with knowing that I gave up. I quit on my brother when he needed my belief in him the most. After I packed a black dress and black pants, I spent the rest of the night with my mind racing. Was he alive? Was he in pain? Was he in the snow, bleeding to death? Was he thinking of us? Was he saying goodbye? Were animals picking at his dead body, unaware their dinner was a life so cherished and so very missed?"

Lissy loved her brother Mark with equal intensity, and she flew home nearly every weekend to be with him during his terminal illness. As her brother's disease ravaged his body, she was a bulwark of support, dignity, and humor. Her maturity has come at a costly price. Despite some tragic circumstances, Lissy keeps on laughing.

XVII

THE LANGUAGE OF SURVIVAL:
STAYING THE COURSE

UNDERNEATH MY KING-SIZE BED lies the history of my children in four plastic boxes, forty-eight inches by ten inches, which encompasses thirty-five years of being a mother. Four different names are scrawled in green magic marker ink on the container lids to distinguish and differentiate each precious life. Inside those boxes are randomly crammed-together contents which include announcements of their births, pediatrician visits, dates of vaccines, report cards, letters from church camps, assorted announcements, programs from piano recitals, swimming and water polo ribbons and medals, college acceptance letters, and dozens of school photos.

Newspaper clippings are beginning to fade in son Jeremy's box. That is what I observed when I pulled from beneath the bed, his life story box. I looked inside and reflected on an astounding survivor—a young man who has surpassed many of my restrained, envisioned goals for his life.

One particularly dramatic photo shows Jeremy on the front page of the Los Angeles Times, clinging precariously to the slippery, sheer rock of a waterfall ledge in the Big Tujunga Canyon. A grimace of a smile captures his tenacity under extreme pressure. Breaking headline news repeatedly reported the waning hope of finding him alive after three days of exposure in a freezing wilderness. On the third day after his disappearance, a decision was made by the rescue teams to call off the helicopter teams at 4:00 PM. Outside, a blackened sky matched the tenseness of my mood. Hope struggled and faltered within me. Now, four years later, I continue to celebrate the persistence and endurance of a man who has been presented with enormous life challenges.

My husband, Steve, and I learned quickly to appreciate the gift of this son when he entered this world, eight weeks prematurely, and was immediately rushed from being delivered at Verdugo Hospital by ambulance to a large neonatal intensive care unit at Los Angeles Children's Hospital. During the late 1970's, premature infants were cared for in sterile incubators. Within two weeks, Jeremy arrived home to meet two older, excited brothers. For the following sixteen years, he was our delight. In school, at play, and on any athletic field, people were instantly drawn to his positive inquisitive nature.

By age seventeen, Jeremy began to struggle and change dramatically. One signal was his sudden withdrawal from his childhood friends. This happened after not being chosen to play on the high school baseball team. For years, he did not speak of that incident. Even now, we all wince when we are reminded of his disappointment. There are wounds etched in his heart. Gradually, Jeremy switched to water sports and excelled at water polo.

It is distressing to witness the happy disposition of a child change into a quarrelsome, reclusive, introverted teen. Psychological intervention was not particularly helpful. We tried to clarify why he was now so unhappy with his life and we looked for signals to indicate substance abuse. Sometimes he sat and sulked on the weekend. Learning in advanced classes no longer held his focused attention. Increasingly, Jeremy wanted to live freely in the outdoors, and he demonstrated this preference by sleeping on our back lawn.

Jeremy appeared happiest whenever he could pursue unconventional paths of dangerous excitement. One time, he hiked to the summit of a mountain in flip-flop shoes. Over a school break, he took off with a buddy and drove straight through to Utah without informing us that he was leaving. We all experienced distress and tensions escalated. I resented having such an unpleasant home life. When Jeremy made an abrupt decision to drop out of La Canada High School three months before graduation, we reacted with rage and fury.

As a family souvenir, our dear friend Paul created a newspaper-style article for our guests to read at a Bon Voyage party we threw for Jeremy:

Jeremy Galton Heads For Belize

Jeremy Galton, youngest son of a prominent La Canada family is going on a summer service project in the subtropical country of Belize with The Christian Environmental Association. The declared mission of this established organization is to build an educational and housing facility for American college students who will spend a semester of their college experience learning about rain forest ecology, and at the same time working to preserve the largest barrier reef in the world. Jeremy will be a part of a site development team, which will prepare the research center, housing, and laboratory facilities for the students and staff who will begin arriving in the near future. Jeremy has long been interested in learning about endangered lands. This will be his first opportunity to actually be on site at a project of such magnitude. In the summer of 1994, Jeremy completed a rigorous three-week survival course in the High Sierras, which further inspired him to pursue his dream.

Jeremy went off to Belize, where he learned about construction and absorbed an appreciation for family and life. In a letter home, he wrote:

My Dear Family,

How much I love you! How I appreciate you. Oh, how I long to be in your presence. When I explore virgin caves, walk on Mayan trails, look for medicinal plants, drive the workers home, build relationships in foreign languages and customs, converse with Kirk in risky, liberating talks, and most of all, when I am alone. I reflect on the silent air, the singing birds, and the wind rustling through the forest. I am not afraid to be alone. For I trust God, and solitude is inner fulfillment. I am filled with the Spirit. I spent so much time walking in circles, looking... trying to satisfy my flesh. And then, I stopped. For it is in solitude that we experience God - the cravings of our heart. The thunder of silence overwhelms me, conquers my flesh, and creates a sanctuary inside of me. This is a place of deep peace. I pray everyday for God to expose characteristics of my life that hold me back from coming closer to His truth. I find myself taking incredible risks, making astonishing leaps of faith. But, I tell you...I never find myself stuck in a rut.

Love,
Jeremy

Our son's activities then ranged from working with this Christian environmental association in Belize to hiking on the Appalachian Trail where he became certified as a white water raft instructor. Tennis, rugby, skiing, swimming, water polo, hiking all seemed to demand his participation and expertise. Above all else, his single great passion was mountain biking. It appeared that he was inextricably bound to rigorous physical activity.

One idea we agreed upon was for Jeremy to receive his high school proficiency certificate. After returning from Belize, Jeremy decided to apply to a college in the Philadelphia area. Respectable grades and excellent SAT scores were faxed off to college and several days later, we were hugging him good-bye. Some problems and challenges continued to baffle us as parents but our relationship appeared so much closer. His manic symptoms troubled us—we wondered about Jeremy's sound judgment. Why did he manifest this deeply ingrained need to master the peak of each new mountain he climbed? No one understood this adrenaline rush to pursue so many adventures except Jeremy, who rarely offered explanations for any strange behavior.

On January 10, 2001, Jeremy agreed to meet me to shop for a winter jacket before he headed back to the Philadelphia area to begin his senior year of college. But he did not show up. The impulsive decision that he made was to take a mountain bike ride with one of his older brothers, Brad. Both of them are skilled hikers, dedicated to serious mountain biking and shared a mutual bond of greeting exciting adventure. Neither of them took the usual precautions to plan for inclement weather or to bring rations of food. They wore thin shirts and shorts. Glorious scenery and forested vistas greeted them on their eight-mile ride deep into the canyons of the Angeles Crest Forest. Abruptly, the trail ended at the foot of the peak. Fast moving clouds and thunder suddenly threatened a blackened sky. Sheets of freezing rain pelted down on their bare legs. Dense fog unexpectedly furled itself around the mountaintop. Despite the absence of visibility, Jeremy yearned to master another mountain summit. Yelling a challenge to his brother to scramble up the remaining two thousand feet—in order to sign their names on a register—he bolted forward on foot.

Later, Brad tearfully confessed that he reluctantly acquiesced to Jeremy's insistent demand. Temperatures plummeted rapidly in the icy storm. Heavy fog separated the brothers. Wisely, Brad decided to leave the mountain and seek assistance. He left a note on Jeremy's bike demanding that Jeremy quickly descend.

It was a long eight-mile descent against the wind to seek emergency help. Within a short time, sheriffs arrived and eventually a hundred teams of search and rescue experts responded to the crisis. Because of the severity of the storm, rescuers and helicopters were halted from beginning the search. The following two days, rescuers scoured these remote canyons to no avail. Jeremy's father and two brothers along with friends, set out on an exhausting search that proved futile.

Suffering arrived at our doorpost. It was humbling to accept ourselves as sufferers. Hours dragged on as the winter storm raged outside. Intimate friends—prayerful companions—kept a vigil with me as we waited in hope. Years of faith and trust helped me to discover a hidden crevice in my heart, some place between terror and trust. Jan, Lisa, Anita, Claudia and Pastor Chuck kept watch with me. Pauline and Laurie also provided comfort. We prayed this Psalm, a paraphrase of Psalm 91, from *Psalms for a Pilgrim People*, by James Cotter:

Yes, with a faith that moves mountains
Still do I trust in my God.
I shall never know lasting harm,
Whatever the testing ordeal.
With my own eyes I shall see
Your judgment and mercy, O God.
Because I have said,
"Oh, God, you are my hope:

you are my refuge and stronghold,"
no great evil shall overwhelm me,
no final destruction crush me.

A friend had written a note to Jeremy before he left for Belize. I quote her because this was our prayer when he was lost:

Your Bible and the promise of Psalm 91 are all you need to take with you. Verse 14 says: "Because he loves me," says the Lord, "I will rescue him; I will protect him, for he acknowledges my name."

Verse 15 continues. "He will call upon me, and I will answer him; I will be with him in trouble, I will deliver him and honor him.

Many accounts in newspapers and magazines have described his ordeal as a miraculous rescue of the twenty-three year old avid outdoorsman, lost for three days in snowy, rugged, mountainous terrain, battling thirst, hunger, and blizzard conditions while maintaining a strong determination to stay alive.

Later Jeremy confessed to us, "I felt death real close. I'm not used to struggling to survive."

We are grateful to the helicopter pilot, who at the end of the third day, spotted a footprint in a streambed, rushed to the spot, and located a cold weary man waving to his rescuers.

My admiration remains strong for Jeremy as I have witnessed him endure confusing pain the past few years. His path of persistence now is to weather an emotional storm intact. This time is vastly different.

We accompany Jeremy as he walks down another sharp descent and will walk beside him as he climbs again to new heights. We support his efforts to finish college or to pursue whatever path may call him. He is learning the merits of persistence. He clings to the path rather than focusing on the precipice.

Jeremy is a wise teacher and helps us accept and compensate for deficits and losses in life. He is beginning to recover and I am proud of him and honor his dreams and hopes. During the vigil four years ago, a friend and I sorted through the memorabilia box and laughed at a post card sent from Jeremy from summer camp when he was about ten:

Dear Dad,
Having a good time... went on an opstical cors today.

Love,
J.R.

I remain optimistic that Jeremy will survive many other obstacle courses.

In creating a portrait of Jeremy, I am awed by both the joy and the pain of being in each other's lives. Jeremy has shown me how to face the shadow side of life. Sometimes this means accepting the unwanted, less desirable qualities in our lives. When we eventually get to the place where we accept those negative characteristics, we can develop a more compassionate understanding of our wholeness as well as our brokenness.

My friend, Carol, who encouraged me to write as a way of speaking about my relationship with God, explained to me that I might consider that, "it is my destiny to be shattered."

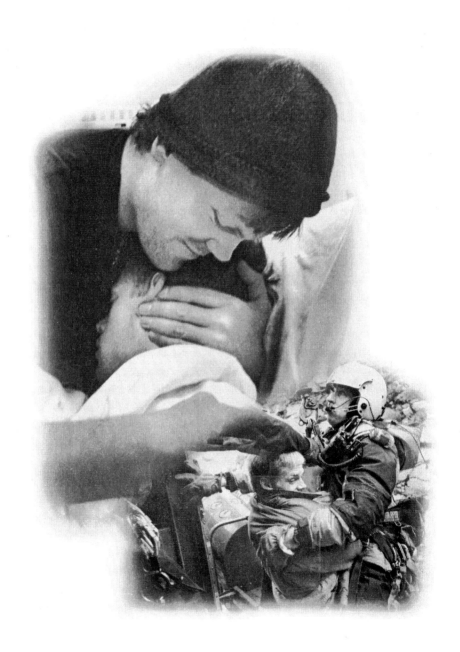

XVIII

THE LANGUAGE OF TRUST:
THE TWO VINES

DANCING IN THE WARM SUMMER BREEZE this
morning are intertwined vines swaying back and forth in a
lazy tempo. One vine is covered in deep indigo blue
flowers. Wide open, they resemble miniature umbrellas.
This day will pass, and the faded flowers will fold like tiny
Japanese party favors as they drop down on the driveway.
Sister vine has the appearance of ruffled heartleaves, on
which are extended curly tendrils growing in every
direction almost like unruly hair.

Looking intently, very carefully, I spotted several newly
formed clumps of celery-colored grapes. No grapes had
appeared the past two years; instead, morning glories
overtook the grape vines. Crushed like grapes after the
harvest, we are still fermenting in our pain and loss. That
day marked the third anniversary of Mark's diagnosis.

Four years ago, I first discovered the grape vine splayed
against an old brick wall hidden in the shrubbery behind
the garage. It must have been here over fifty years, I
thought. During springtime, Pittesporum bushes perfume

this area with an orange blossom fragrance. July 2001 was my first noticing of the clumps of grapes forming on the mass of tangled vines. Until then, there was only an old apricot tree with popcorn blossoms promising fruit later in the season.

This space in my garden has become sacred to me. Here is where I imagine, pray, grieve, write notes, drink my morning coffee, and reflect on my life. In my garden, I discover nourishment and healing. My garden often speaks to me of the ways God may be caring for and tending me. For years, I have desired for my garden to flourish and thrive in order that I can do the same. Near the wall of vines stands a Japanese maple tree which lends some shade to the "water feature."

"Did you turn off the water feature?" my husband or I ask each other on entering the house after sipping a glass of wine out there on summer evenings. I don't know why we couldn't think of a better name than calling our fountain the "water feature."

Once a fantasy in my imagination, and later a sketch scrawled on a legal pad by a good friend, the water feature design was built the summer before the grapes. Against the back wall of this semi-circular, brick structure are three small apertures, through which water drops into a tiny pool. When that pool is full, the water spills into an arc of water two feet deep. By early summer, white iceberg roses and a boxwood hedge cover most of the fountain wall. My soul becomes soothed by the sound of the water falling.

September 2000 marked the inauguration date for the water feature, a fitting backdrop for an engagement celebration dinner in our yard. An unanticipated light drizzle began to fall, so Lissy quickly altered the plan and moved the tables under the eaves of the patio.

Mark and his fiancé, Shelby, were as always, radiant and gracious. Excitement crackled like electricity as guests chatted over a festive French dinner. The celebrated couple sat with their friends inside the dining room at the "kids" table. The wedding, planned for the following summer, would take place at a vineyard destination and the festivities would continue for three days. Toasting late into that evening, no amount of drizzle or chill would have marred that enchanted gathering. Sweet grapes were in the wine that night.

Gainey Vineyard was a spectacular venue for the wedding eleven months later. A pepper tree arch framed the dear faces of the adorable couple. Guests left the weekend toting jars of homemade olive tapenade and rich memories. The newly wedded couple, Mr. and Mrs. Mark Galton, left for a sailing honeymoon in Australia. Back home, we continued to taste the sweet grapes until they soured after the September 11th attacks.

I watched that autumn as the grapes by the water feature dried into tiny, black, hard nodules. Nodules were probably beginning to form in Mark's body as well. In a gardening guide, I read the correct procedure to prune back the canes so that more fruit would be produced the following summer. There is a delicate balance on how severe one should prune before damaging the vine. I am reminded of the scripture where Christ speaks about the vine and the branches. Christ likens the metaphor to a spiritual life in which believers are grafted into God's life. People are compared to a vine that needs to be regularly pruned. This metaphor suggests that people live a life in God as He dwells in the human soul. That mystical relationship is meant to be organic and intimate.

In June 2002, the vine grew but produced no grapes. Recently, I turned the pages in my journal of memories and rediscovered the entry on July 18th. The entry reads:

A busy day seeing clients and facilitating a bereavement group and then the anticipation of meeting Steve for supper at the Star Café.

Steve's voice shook that evening as he began to voice his concerns over Mark's physical appearance as they had met for lunch downtown that day. Later I wrote:

I can't imagine anything really serious happening to Mark. He is robust, an outstanding athlete and has never been sick.

His condition changed rapidly. Two days later, we encouraged him to go to the hospital emergency room. His complaints included persistent pain, inability to sleep, and bloating due to fluid retention. Liver tests came back with a very abnormal interpretation. The next step was for him to be admitted and Mark entered Cedar Sinai Hospital emergency room for an ultrasound and CAT scan of his liver. We felt so emotional. Mark appeared strong in spirit, but the jaundice made him look so vulnerable.

Privately, we listened as he spoke his worst fears. His voice trembled, I thought, when he confessed his worst fear was a possibility of cancer. We reassured him that 33 year-old healthy men don't develop cancer. Attempts to reassure him seemed feeble and inadequate. It was a nerve-wracking wait to hear the results. Steve and Brad were on a business trip back East. Biopsy results were not expected until mid-week.

On Tuesday, I drove down to the hospital by myself. Dr. Wolfe stepped into the hospital room and abruptly asked which family members were present.

"I only want to speak once," he announced curtly. Quickly I paged Shelby and her parents to return from the cafeteria. Those next five minutes altered our lives forever. His words were searing wounds to the heart.

"Take your medical jargon away," I wanted to yell. A tsunami of horror and shock ripped into the scene. A demeanor of calm remained on Mark's face as he was informed that he had adenocarcinoma of the pancreas that had spread to the liver and throughout his intestines. Surgery was not an option.

Distress and disbelief followed with such fierceness that I could not stand. Shelby screamed and sobbed. Our hearts broke and shattered. Total despair rose to the surface. Mark, Shelby and the doctor talked privately about the treatment options. In the waiting room, I looked out the window unable to comprehend how the world was still functioning. Traffic still crept down Sunset Boulevard. People carried shopping bags. *Why hadn't the whole world gone into a frozen shock?*

Is it true that there is a season and a time for every matter under heaven? Certainly there is the time to be born, and then there should follow at least seventy years. Could a healthy, eldest son die at age thirty-three? No, this couldn't be happening to Mark. Life is supposed to be comprehensible. Suffering arrived unbidden, and we could not grasp the loss of self-sufficiency.

As a family, we were determined to match the intensity of Mark's courage and fearlessness with the intensity of our love, support, and prayer. Cheerful cards arrived with our discovery that there are no right words to offer in this kind of crisis. Privately, Steve and I prayed that God would transfer the cancer into our bodies and spare Mark. We wept through the bad times, mourned the anticipated children who would never play in our garden, and prayed that the love of God would see Mark through. "Never lose heart," I repeated to myself as a mantra. The vine, by the water feature still bore no fruit.

I believe in miracles and I personally chose to believe that in the midst of this distress, God would intervene and heal Mark. Our family had been plunged into the suffering caused by Mark's prognosis, but surely, God would respond to our anguish and intervene with a cure. My roots are deeply imbedded in God's history of faithfulness. My answered prayers would testify to the world that our lives bear good fruit. I swore a lot, especially with some good friends.

Shelby informed us that the oncologist stated Mark could not recover. There are no pancreatic survivors. Most live a few months after diagnosis. Mark was already in stage four when diagnosed. I wanted to die when I thought of what was coming. *Would death be the harvest of a parent's life investment into a child?* Shelby asked us to put together a book on he life of Mark. A videographer captured his life on a video that we presented to them on their first wedding anniversary. These were offerings of our spirits and lives together.

There was no lushness or fragrance in my garden. I did not go outside. Nothing flourished. Barrenness. That was all. On July 29th, I wrote in my journal:

> *I find myself constantly reflecting on Mark's remarkable life. His exuberance for living on the mountain peaks endears him to so many people. This is a day when I feel like I am walking through the flames of hell. I don't want to have to relinquish Mark to suffering. He is barely a man and too young to be walking such a treacherous path. My heart is pulverized.*

In the end, our prayers appeared to go unanswered. I had offered to give up my own life, so that Mark's life would be spared. Each of us carried a heavy cross, and the weight of that cross was unbearable.

December 23rd, 2002 also happened to be my husband Steve's 65th birthday. On this sunny day, after visiting with many friends and family the day before, our son Mark left us in his thirty-third year. He had been conscious and spoke precious words to his wife. But words cannot express the searing heartache I felt holding his lifeless body and committing his soul for safe keeping into the Creator's arms. That awful agony of offering Mark back to God shattered me totally.

That next summer, a small morning glory plant began to grow wildly where the grapes had been.

We continued to grieve. Summer 2004 brought a spectacular profusion of blue morning glories.

In spring 2005, on his birthday, I noticed the grape vine was flourishing, and wrote Mark a grateful response:

Dear Mark,

Today, you would be thirty-six years old, and we would be celebrating with you. We are proud of you, dear first son. We never thought you would go away. You have always been bigger than life. I am still crushed and heartbroken and fragmented without you. For me, you have always been the symbol of joy and adventure, playfulness and vibrancy, vigor and courage, determination and movie star good looks. Our shining light is gone. In its stead I carry a bleakness of heart and a million stories that make me smile.

I am grateful to have experienced such a man as you. Because of you, I am inspired to help other children who are suffering. I refuse to give up my faith in the power of love or in the wisdom of a God whom I have always trusted. There is no choice but to submit to the sustainer of life. We watched your precious body decay until your soul and spirit had to take flight, to be released from the cancer-ravaged container. I must still believe in God and find reasons to live. How you lived until your last moment gives me courage to face whatever is coming now. Dad and I have crossed over the threshold of fear and terror.

Human life is so precious. We no longer worry about our deaths. You died with grace and left us love. You were remarkable and I imagine that your perfected spirit soars. Our faith gives us hope that you crossed over first and we are not frightened to follow. Your smiling face is all around us but the ache and pain of losing you is scarcely dulled. I will love you forever.

Mom

Like the harvested grape, my spirit is crushed into fragments of memories and I need to be renewed each day. I am back watching my blooming vines thrive in this summer of 2005. In the cool and pleasant place by the water feature, I read this passage from Hosea 14:7 as I wonder about the vines:

They shall again live beneath my shadow, they shall flourish like a garden; they shall blossom like the vine, their fragrance shall be like the wine of Lebanon.

Maybe the two vines remind me of the inner garden I need to cultivate more carefully. I want to bloom again and feel the beauty of a new season after the severe pruning. I have been quoting a scripture, Jeremiah 17:10, daily for seven years that I believe God gave as an assurance to me:

But blessed is the woman who trusts in the Lord,
whose confidence is in Him.
She will be like a tree planted by the water
that sends out its roots by the stream.
It does not fear when heat comes;
its leaves are always green.
It has no worries in a year of drought
and never fails to bear fruit.

That terrible day in December, we left behind a part of ourselves. I believe, however, that as we emerge from the treacherous grief, God is still bearing us up. Even though our known life seems totally upside down, there are signs of newness— the two vines have flourished, the roots of the tree have grown stronger, and yellow birds bathe in the glory of the water feature.

XIX

THE LANGUAGE OF THANKFULNESS: PEOPLE THAT LOOK LIKE JESUS

ABOUT TEN YEARS AGO, I was invited to be a facilitator for a newly forming group at La Canada Presbyterian Church. "Companions for the Journey" consists of a covenant group of persons who gather one long evening every month, in a shared desire to listen for God in their own lives as well as the other community members.

Often, the question is asked: "How does God speak to us in the moment and over time?" One aspect of listening intentionally for what may be God's promptings includes journaling about phrases from Scripture and recording the sensations of powerful feelings. Through *Companions*, my faith journey has expanded. In that protected environment, we practice prayerful presence, authenticity, and a respect for each individual's receptivity to God.

Lisa Myers, a revered spiritual director, author, and teacher, and Rev. Judy Durff, Pastor of Spiritual Formation at La Canada Presbyterian Church, provide excellent ongoing supervision and teaching for us. This spiritual nurture and guidance is transforming, and it teaches me about a whole new way of praying Scripture. As we delve deeper into the observing and reflections, we wonder whether they were indeed invitations from God.

Frequently, this could be translated as listening for a new way of being or doing. About five years ago, I began to hear a question forming: "Can you drink this cup?" Each time I listened to that question, I wept. Sometimes, I simply felt over the edge with the demands and complexities of life. One of the most stirring parts of being an "elder" in my congregation was the pure joy of serving the bread and wine during communion to the gathered body of faith. But this question came to be disturbing and left me uncomfortable. In the perplexity of that terrifying question, I knew that I was being strengthened to travel a deep valley. None of us, intentionally, invite a lashing storm into our faltering paths.

A sense came into my heart, that what I would drink might be bitter wine. This could be a test for which my faith, hope, courage, and confidence would fail. Enough tribulation had entered our home, and what I desired was peace. Yes, I felt quite willing and eager to drink sweet wine. Please God, let my cup be fabricated of fine porcelain and steaming with black tea. *Will I be faithful?* I wondered, in "the breaking of bread and the drinking of the cup" in whatever direction I was led.

Anticipating a death and then surviving the actual death of a son reduces a family to an almost primitive survival state. I wrote in my journal on August 9, 2002:

All of us are dealing with our anxieties and fears differently. Cancer is horrible. I cannot and will not ask the "Why" question. Nothing makes sense. Mark responds positively to everyone. Shelby is so loving. We search for a hope beyond anything that cancer can do.

Two days later, I turned back to my journal. For about two months, I recorded my thoughts and then could no longer organize a single sentence. This entry was important because it was Mark and Shelby's first wedding anniversary:

Although the hospital did not want to release him, Mark managed to check himself out. We delivered three-dozen Leonitas roses from Jacob Maarse Florist to The Inn at Playa Del Rey. Their room faced out on the wetlands and, from their balcony, one could see the tips of sailboats fluttering in the sea breeze. It was a teary night for me, until Mark and Shelby telephoned to say it was the happiest day of their lives. They are two soul mates on a rocky sea, facing an unknown destiny. We wonder with amazement that they find so much love together. Mark is fighting a courageous battle. Steve and I just wish we could do it for him. Mark continues to live a brave life. There are shadows of terror lurking in the rest of us.

Words cannot express the combination of ripping heartache, anguish, and wearisome fatigue that marked those months. However, I saw our son inspire us. We also witnessed the unselfish love of friends who cared for us daily. The truth about the sacredness of community speaks loudly, especially in perilous crisis. Friends learned and practiced caregiving. They enhanced our ability to persevere in order for us to keep our souls and our sanity intact. The friends came to illumine the total darkness. Christian friends became our sustenance as we clung for dear life in terrible depression. "God, do not forsake us," I prayed.

The companionship of friends saved us. This pilgrimage knew no precedent. Compassionate prayer flowed towards us. Friends entered into a deep solidarity as an expression of God's love for us and for Mark. Even when the concerns and burdens in your life seem unbearable, and you think there is no more endurance in you, these burdens may be borne by those friends who travel on your journey as witnesses to your deepening relationship with God. To a suffering person, healing words are a potent medicine. I clung, personally to words of comfort. In the shadow of Mark's approaching death, I also experienced silent prayer as efficacious.

When I no longer could journal, I made notations on scraps of paper of those who brought loving concern and precious refuge into our lives and their heartfelt acts. God, I believe, has held unto us through the tender consolation of these friends. They have been heart gifts.

Some, even more than the others who were of great comfort, shined especially bright and picked us up during "the shattering." I offer you now my thank you notes so I don't have to mail them:

Dear Jan,

Thank you for being there daily with me for 159 days on my couch, for demonstrating by your own journey that we are not victims, for keeping us calm and guarding me against terror, for encouraging words, for endless listening, for sending Mark and Shelby care packages, for countless acts of love and tenderness, for the love feast the night of the diagnosis, for your common sense and the gift of processing life and for your steadfast, unwavering faith in God. Thank you for sitting under the afghan with me. Thank you for showing me that survivors can someday thrive again. Thank you for demonstrating racy alternatives to using the "F" word when you detest what someone has said in the grocery store—or not said—as they fled around the corner to avoid me.

Dear Claudia,

Thank you for accepting me as your sister in Christ, for never once being afraid to enter into the center of our pain, for flowers and back door surprises, for hundreds of prayers, for babysitting me on Fridays at lunch, for being a part of the Monday support group, for loving children, and for not only understanding the importance of a good place for the memorial reception, but for providing your lovely home.

Dear Susan,

Thank you for getting the whole thing right, for having the wisdom to speak God's truth in gentle ways, for describing the vision in which you imagined that Mark would be ecstatic to arrive in Heaven, for lunches in my backyard, for bearing the pain with us and never shrinking away from our despair, for giving Mark the childhood memories of Pine Oak Ranch, for knowing how to hold a shattered person. Thank you for introducing us to another sacred place where we continue to be held in love.

Dear Britta,

Thank you for just being wonderful you, for comforting massages, for bringing us an entire Swedish meatball and lingoberry dinner, for not being upset when we left Marielle's wedding early, for sharing your adorable granddaughter, for not acting annoyed when I confided that I didn't care whether I lived. Thank you for honesty in our communication and the lack of judgment.

Dear Margaret,

Thank you for all your telecare and for looking out for the welfare of our other sons. You are our auntie, a trusted and wise woman. You are the only person to have sent e-mail offering to take out the trash and clean out the refrigerator, as well as go buy stamps at the post office.

Dear Cathie,

Thank you for coming over to be with us when I was terribly afraid, for remaining patient with me through all my irritability, and for all your honesty in admitting that you really weren't sure what to say. Admitting that to someone is a powerful link. Your confession that you did not know what to say made me desire the safety of being with you.

Dear Dianne,

Thank you for your Saturday morning notes which came out of your "garden prayers." Thank you for being a silent and powerful presence.

Dear Judy,

Thank you for the heroic efforts you made in resuscitation and executive thinking. Panic attacks do mimic heart attacks. Despite the embarrassment, it was right to go to the emergency room. Thank you for being assertive with an insensitive doctor.

Dear Robin,

Thank you for choosing to fly out to California for the memorial service. That was an act of pure grace. Thank you for the dozens of telephone calls.

Dear Ann,

Thank you for your willingness to spend spiritually nourishing and empathic time every Monday for months, for the tears you wept over our anguish, for kindness and remembering the long history of our friendship, and for checking in on the phone so often.

Dear Ceil,

Thank you for all the ways you honor our family. You brought food on fine china, memories stretching over decades, and tender holding. Thank you for coming over immediately on Christmas Eve to be near.

Dear Chris,

Thank you for always caring about our kids, for regularly calling, for listening without judgment to my abominable expletives, for placing a strengthening hand on my shoulder when we tried attending church, for holding my hand in public, and for the familiarity of your expression, "What can I say?"

Dear Elza,

    Thank you for continuous support, for showing up spontaneously on bad days when we lost hope, for countless pots of homemade soup, for listening endlessly, for being there the night of Mark's diagnosis, for being there again the night of his death, for denying yourself and leaving a surprise Christmas breakfast at our back door, and for all your prayers. Thank you for knowing what to do to support a friend. Thank you for movie therapy.

Dear Jeanie,

    Thank you for loving me and for loving children everywhere. Thank you for tea and scones and hugs and for bringing love into our home on a desperate Christmas Eve afternoon.

Dear Karen,

    Thank you for all the telecare and allowing me to disintegrate into your arms when you returned to California. Thank you for being a saint who wears red shoes, purple dresses, and smiles a lot. You always make yourself accessible. How we cherish our long years of knowing you.

Dear Pauline,

    Thank you for not judging my negativity, for loving everyone in our family, for calling constantly, for calling me "sweetie", for reminding me that life goes on, for not criticizing me when I told you how horribly we were doing, and for sitting beside me when I made the matching scrapbooks for Mark and Brad of their childhood.

Dear Carol,

    Thank you for your selfless love poured out extravagantly, for leaving notes and gifts at the back door, for driving me to my job when I was having a panic attack, for making the art of hammocking a verb and for climbing in the hammock with me, for running endless errands, for printing the memorial program, and for treating me as a favorite, cherished sister. I will forever be humbled by your expansive willingness to care. Thank you for staying with me through the shattering time, and for celebrating my being glued together when I was finally able to place a chipped piece of china into the mosaic art piece.

Dear Jackie,

Thank you for your prayers, for modeling appropriate expressions of sincerity, for understanding the uniqueness of a first born child, and for our long history based on a shared faith.

Dear Laurie,

Thank you for staying the course, and never being reluctant to be in the eye of the storm as a hovering angel, for so many Friday nights of chocolate desserts and good wine, for sensitivity, for hugs, for your patience, for countless dinners, for faithfulness in friendship, for loving my family, and for being present when the emotions seemed unendurable. Thank you for bringing chocolate chip cookies to Lissy before Mark's memorial service. You are unique. You sprinkle joy into the hearts of those who mourn and make them smile despite their sadness.

Dear Lisa,

Thank you for writing the blessing for the service and for demonstrating that "You are loved beyond imagining." Your tangible love helped me affirm the presence of God's spirit with us. Thank you for staying when they laid Mark's body in the ground. Thank you for your willingness to shed tears with me.

Dear Bobbi,

Thank you for becoming sensitively involved instead of turning away, for recording such loving and helpful telephone messages, for going out for Mexican food and listening, for demonstrating a sweet voice of love when I railed, and for opening your home and extending hospitality. I felt almost human, being invited for pizza. Thank you for staying cool and for not fearing the anger, which accompanied the helplessness.

Dear Judy,

Thank you for your ability to hold in balance a pastor's as well as a friend's heart, for weeping and walking with me on a path of deep sorrow, for rushing to my home when I became afraid and overwhelmed, for understanding the spiritual reality of a pain-bearing God, for your sensitivity to each member of Shelby's family and for writing a thoughtful homily. Thank you for realizing that a prayer chapel should be unlocked. Thank you for helping us lament. Thank you for not fearing the desolate cry of a mother who could not save her child.

Dear Michael,

Thank you for hours of talking with us, for your compassion, for caring so much about family dynamics, for weeping with us over shattered hopes, for laughing when I said the "F…" word so much and then rewarding me with a night at the movies when I had not sworn for three whole days, and for being with us the night Mark died. Thank you for sitting with us, hour after hour, and for not paying an obligatory visit and then rushing off.

Dear Harvey,

Thank you for your perspective on lamenting a son, for sharing your unique perspective on a parent's grief, for respecting and honoring our needs, and for encouraging the celebrations of life which continue.

Dear Mort,

Thank you for performing the graveside service and for finding just the right words to lay Mark to rest, "Good night, sweet prince." Thank you for remembering and for speaking about the history of our two families over those thirty-three years.

Dear Bill,

Thank you for showing up often and telling me the truth about depression and then sitting with me during some rugged hours. Thank you for recognizing the indescribable hurt. Thank you for always being authentic and bringing the bonsai ministry to my doorstep. Thank you for allowing us to lean on you afterward.

Dear Paul,

Thank you for not shrinking away from something so uncomfortable, for taking us very seriously when we admitted we needed help from old friends while Mark went through the process of dying, for saving us seats at church, for introducing us to the Evensong service, for passing on the peace that sustains, and for remembering how much we are nourished by dinner in your home.

Dear Don,

Thank you for carefully listening to Steve each week, for not becoming disturbed when we stumbled, for sharing your personal, painfully sad story of a brother dying, and for inviting us into your home and creating safety and comfort.

Dear Jim,

Thank you for not hesitating to be present in a situation that felt so out of control, for serious listening when we asked for help, and for providing some socializing to ward off some of the sense of isolation.

Dear Hank,

Thank you for your openness and genuineness, for treating us as normal people when we acted crazy, and for hanging out so much when you were already busy.

Dear Tom,

Thank you for your sincerity, for your integrity, for your willingness to be the first person to pray for us, for your capability in helping us confront our fears realistically, for understanding the proud heart of a father, and for coming to our home and preparing us for the shock and denial that we might actually lose Mark.

Dear Kent,

Thank you for introducing us to the world of anti-depressants and sleeping medication, for sharing your personal stash of pills, for talking to our children in ways that made them trust you, for bringing your compassion into the heart of our deepest suffering, for simply sitting with us for countless hours while we sobbed and struggled, and for locating Jeremy to offer sad news.

Dear Bob,

Thank you for your fearlessness in delivering tragic news, for your effective listening skills, for demonstrating so much lay pastoral care, for never caring whether we were in a lousy mood, and for treating us to a special dinner remembering that we needed to be surrounded by love

Dear Frank,

Thank you for helping us remember humorous stories about being neighbors, for raising caring children who came and wept with me, for being a solid man, and for spending time with us.

Dear Gary,

Thank you for lending me your wife for five months, for opening up your home and garden for the reception, for appreciating the importance of being a good father, and for understanding the spirit of an adventuresome risk taker.

Dear Doug,

Thank you for taking time to go to Steve's office and support and pray for him, for truly understanding pastoral care, and for helping us to begin to let go of wishes and dreams that cannot be.

Dear Chuck,

Thank you for coming close when the anguish hit, for coming to the hospital when Mark was diagnosed, for always coming to our home when we needed you as friend and pastor, for your steady faith in traversing life's mountains and valleys, for helping us release Mark's spirit into the hands of God, for honoring Shelby's and our family in your comments, and for reminding us all that death is the threshold doorway to resurrection.

These are poignant memories that I have collected from experiencing the depth and sheer wonder of unselfish love. I will never comprehend all that happened, but I do know that because of these people that resemble Jesus, strength has been offered to stand firm in the storm. On a tough path, despite markers, amazing love kept us steadfast. Tested to the limit, vulnerable and fragile to the core, God knew and gave us the kind of love that endures.

Certainly, we suffered greatly, but I know that we will always remember that unselfish and warm affection that allowed us to feel so cherished during "the shattering."

XX

THE LANGUAGE OF FAITH:
REARRANGING THE SHATTERED PIECES

I USED TO WEAR a diamond necklace around my neck. Steve gave me the necklace as an anniversary gift and I felt so proud to own such an exquisite piece of jewelry. As the anticipated hopes and expectations of my handsome family shattered into a billion pieces after Mark's death, I exchanged the diamond necklace for a cross, which I wear on a gold chain.

So many things have shifted in my life, and I continue to look for a firm footing as I did after the fall into the basement. Some of the people who stood by me in the deepest yearnings and disappointments have shielded me from further hurt and helped me sift through all the broken pieces. These women, through their actions and words, became for me the radiant spiritual gems which adorn my heart. They are significant jewels strung together in the softest lining of my soul. Each one of them wears and has carried a cross of her own.

Artis, a sixty-year-old man, was dying at home from bone cancer. His wife requested the presence of a Stephen minister. Stephen ministers are trained and skilled in being empathic listeners. Our pastor, Chuck Osburn, and I offered to serve communion to him at home. Artis had been reconnecting with his spiritual roots during his illness and I wanted to extend a tangible sign of the love we felt for him. I baked a loaf of Irish soda bread, covered it with a white linen cloth, and set the loaf on a pewter plate inscribed with the word *love* all around the rim. Gathered around his bed, we poured the grape juice into a pewter pitcher.

Everything was perfectly prepared for this love feast. Everyone present knew that Artis would soon be making a spiritual pilgrimage of his own. Suddenly, he motioned me with his finger to move closer so that he could whisper in my ear. Placing my hand on his shoulder, I bent down to hear his barely audible words. "This...this helping, you must help the dying. God needs you to do that." These were holy moments.

Two weeks later, Artis died. I remember sitting with his grieving wife, Glenda, and his used-up body for several hours until the undertaker arrived. I recall how palpable the density of spirit life felt in that bedroom. We opened the sliding door to welcome in the cool night air and acknowledge the departure of his spirit from his body.

Those words he spoke continued to influence me, and I became a certified grief counselor. Soon after, the instructor invited me to help facilitate a bereavement group at Glendale Adventist Hospital. That opportunity gradually developed into an associate chaplain position.

In addition to visiting patients, I was counseling about twenty clients a week. Between the years of 1998 and 2001, I logged over four thousand counseling hours. It is a unique privilege to sit with someone and be invited into the source of his or her wound. Working in a chaplain's office afforded the opportunity to assist clients in viewing the integration of their core values and their spirituality as resources in confronting problems. I couldn't wait to arrive at the hospital each day.

The Board of Behavioral Sciences in Sacramento had already approved my experience and I was scheduled within three weeks to sit for the state-licensing exam. Then Mark was diagnosed.

Sadly, in that tumultuous season of grief, I could not concentrate well enough to reschedule the exam and I let the time lapse. Such is the stranglehold of grief.

An unexpected opportunity came when Dr. Paul Peterson, longstanding scholar and expert in missions, invited me to go to Londrina, Brazil. Then, the September 11th attacks came along and some of the participants decided against boarding a plane due to the seriousness of terrorist warnings. But Margaret Mitchell, a four-foot-ten-inch stick of intellectual dynamite, agreed to join the short-term mission group. Margaret and I taught a fifty-member class through a curriculum based on family systems and pastoral care. Already close friends, we busily prepared our lesson plans prior to our departure. I loved hearing Portuguese spoken and spent hours listening to Berlitz tapes.

I was disturbed to see the dominance of male clergy in Brazil; only a few women attended our weeklong seminar. We were gratified to stress the importance of women being equally involved in ministry. Learning to be flexible in a foreign environment was a key lesson gleaned from that experience. Going to Brazil opened my eyes to new possibilities and the conviction that people are saved one by one.

I find myself drawn to people and places that have a "Jesus imprint" on their hands. What I discovered in this sad time is that in God, we are all one. It is a given grace that we belong to each other. We may grapple with tribulations and suffering, some of which is simply unavoidable. But we are all woven together in love. This is what intimate community looks like to me. My sense of belonging is embedded in friendship, and I have always desired to be God's friend as well. In the Old Testament, I read these reassuring words from Jeremiah 31:3 and Isaiah 43:1:

I have loved you with an everlasting love...
I have called you by name, you are mine.

Like the vines in my garden, the lives of my friends in "the group" have been intertwined. This sisterhood is composed of seven women who are exceptionally creative, energetic and loving. Britta organized the group fifteen years ago with the "explicit purpose" of reading a book. I can't remember if we ever actually completed reading an entire book. Laurie, Karen, Elza, Jeanie, and Britta meet weekly in my home. Shirley has since moved, but she attends when she's back in town. We know each other like old bathrobes and slippers that we refuse to give up. There are no secrets between us and nothing is off-limits in our sharing. We have sat together, howling with laughter, and we have been light for each other in darkness and the shadow of death. In the midst of living busy days, the group cultivated authentic friendship and blessed each other with a sense of the unconditional affirmation of God. Each one is a surprise and a reminder from God to keep on living and loving.

Sheila Crabtree is a crucial gift, a soul mate, a woman with great integrity, who walked straight into my heart and life. One evening in March 2004, I had spoken along with Margaret in a continuing education class at Stephen Ministry training. The topic chosen was about complicated grief. Fifteen months had already passed since Mark's death. In my confused state of pain, I never thought that great surges of emotion would flood me. Death had caused so much vulnerability and I wasn't stable enough to avoid weeping. In fact, I cried throughout the presentation. Not much helped restore emotional balance in the awful void of missing my son. Sheila approached me afterwards, and I saw in her tear-filled eyes the gaze of kindred understanding. *Could she be in the middle of struggle?* I wondered.

A few days later, Sheila quietly slipped a note into my hands while we attended a Companions monthly gathering. Inside was a thank you about the disastrous talk and a check made out to a ministry in Kenya called The Shepherd's Home. The Shepherd's Home offers a sanctuary for twenty-five girls who have lost their parents and other family members to AIDS in the impoverished slums of Nairobi. To help with the AIDS pandemic, two couples, long-term friends and Fuller Seminary graduates, jointly committed to respond to the plight of these girls. They responded through a world development organization that Drs. Jackie and Doug Millham founded in the early 1980's called Discover The World.

The initial focus of this ministry has been responding to girls because of their unique vulnerability to prostitution and AIDS. From Scripture, the commands, "Love your neighbor" and "Feed my sheep" kept repeating in my mind. The first night I heard about Shepherd's Home, I felt compelled to go the following summer.

On the church patio, one day in the spring of 2004, I asked, "Sheila, would you consider going to Africa with me and the team that's leaving in August?"

"I'll think about it," she smiled back as she disappeared into the church. That God-timed encounter on "Mission Sunday" was the beginning of a profound friendship.

I still can't believe how that all unfolded. Two women had both sustained devastating grief, were determined to recover and heal, and followed their God-driven instincts to allow the Holy Spirit to guide. Sheila and I traveled together to far away Kenya, fell in love with these precious children, and witnessed the beginning of transformation in their lives. More orphanages are being opened and renovated and are connected to private schools and churches.

Sheila has demonstrated the humility of letting go of some things that truly involve mourning. One of her great strengths is the quality of embracing and being honest about who she really is. Together, on an authentic journey, we have faced the hard reality that there are no soothing fantasies of an idyllic life. She is an exceptional mother and "nana." Sheila is steadfast in her trust in a God that allows us to embrace disappointment and achievements. She is a prime example of a woman who hears "The Word" and immediately receives it with joy. I have watched an inner transformation in Sheila's life as she responds seriously to the call to love her neighbor, which she does compassionately and concretely.

I remember telling Claudia Zentmyer that I did not want to become a bitter martyr. Instead, I needed God's comfort expressed through friends to guide us along the path of deep personal pain. If obtaining a clean scar meant bleeding profusely, I would take that. Claudia understands the loneliness. She is a spiritual director and indeed, was an insightful woman before her formal training. She allowed herself to enter the pain of a grieving person, a mother, coming to terms with her altered self. From the onset of Mark's diagnosis, Claudia spent several hours a week praying with me, talking and eating lunch in our favorite corner table tucked away from the crowd of normal, happy people.

In a time teeming with confusion and uncertainty, she offered the kind of support that allays terrible anxiety. Her gentle presence in my life has had enormous therapeutic value. I am humbled by the strength and gifts I received being held in the sanctuary of Claudia's prayers. God has embraced me through her hugs. Losing a child is every mother's most ghastly nightmare. Claudia wept unabashedly beside me. It was not time that was healing the wound. The hole and the scar felt soothed only when these dear ones sat, sometimes in silence, waiting for signs of new life to appear.

Carol Wawrychuk has the spiritual gift of surprising insight, which she freely offers when she enters into a space that she knows to be truly safe. Intuitively, she knows how to look beyond the surface. She carefully pays attention to what happens in the muddy waters. A teacher by profession, she has taught me the underestimated art of "wasting time" in encountering the mysterious presence of Jesus. We became close friends a few years ago but were acquaintances for twenty years. To Carol, I remain indebted for keeping Lissy clean in her pre-school classroom.

I am indebted to Carol for helping me use loneliness as creative solitude. We have shared both our writing and our vision that the divine would shine through us, working for good in the shattered world. Carol speaks with remarkable honesty. Just when I believed my life to be over, Carol resolved to accompany me on this dreadful path through loss and wracking pain. We would never be "arm in arm" had my life remained unscathed.

Inner solitude and quiet stillness have been unique ways in which we have connected. Quietly rocking on her front porch, we have listened for birds. When I am traveling with Steve, I always know that Carol lights a candle and prays for me at 6:45 AM. We have felt the sunshine warm on our faces as we have attempted to put words on the mystery of our shared faith. I am never afraid to walk around emotionally naked in front of Carol. Her warm companionship is comforting. Sometimes, I arrive home to open a touching handwritten note. She stretches out her hand to me. She is a refuge for me and we offer each other signs of our noticing that we are not alone on our healing paths. We are living reminders to each other that if we turn to God with trusting hearts, we will ultimately be okay. This Loving One, to whom we turn somehow, sustains us in a rich, spiritual friendship. The connection between Carol, God, and me is evidence of the sacramental nature of Christ. God seems to stir up love in us and we are in awe.

I began this book describing a faithful friend, named Jan Roberts, whom I have known for thirty-three years. In a most endearing and unassuming way, she taught me lesson upon lesson. For all this time, she has known my deepest fear of being abandoned by those whom I love. Childhood history prepared me to dread that if I were to be genuinely myself that someone would disapprove and march angrily out of my life forever. Can you imagine the enormous relief of having a friend who may occasionally be disappointed with you but never dreams of severing the friendship? Jan forgives the sin and flaws in people. Her life was bombarded with terrible loss, and I watched her rise courageously from the fiery pit to continue a journey into an uncertain life before her. I remember counting whatever tender mercies we saw in our lives. Jan does not fear questions about her life as a believer. Part of her inspiring obedience is being open to the newness of life. A dedicated gardener, she moves through her English garden waiting for the buds to appear. The full blooming of this friendship is a much-savored gift.

Decades of friendship have proven that Jan is a woman to be trusted. She is brimming over with wisdom and insight and knows important nuances of self-expression. Jan has taught many frustrated novice parents how to hold on and when to let go. Her creative curriculum draws on her own spiritual journey through life. More beautiful than any of her other sterling attributes is her honoring of people's uniqueness. She abandons herself to delighted laughter often. She blesses her aging parents with a nightly ritual. She taught me the art of movie therapy. I have never had to earn her love or her affirmation. *Jan loves me. Imagine that!*

My husband, Steve, is the partner who stood by me in every joy and crisis. He has been an effective listener. Together, we have traveled through life and around the world. Our frequent travels brought glimpses of life elsewhere and we share an ongoing movie playing in our collected memories. As a father, he has relentlessly encouraged our children. As a husband, he has walked solidly through all the peaks and valleys. Steve and I have done the work required to sustain a marriage. Usually, we have been on the right path and understood how to build a home from scratch. I am thankful to be bound in life to this beloved partner and husband.

True community, I believe and have experienced, has its origins and roots in the love God offers. God has overwhelmed me with goodness being part of community. My pastor, Chuck, knows that I have difficulty with the concept of redemptive suffering. *People named Grace shouldn't have to suffer*, I reason and rationalize. I hear a beckoning hope, appearing sometimes only briefly, but it includes a hope of restoration. The stitching together of the life quilt continues. Still, I have received a grace, a promise that the underside of the unfinished fabric of my life is of value to share.

In some sense, I feel as though I am wearing the garment of my life inside out and I am not ashamed for you to touch the worn, faded fabric. The whole along with the holes represent congruence. The label on this imaginary garment reads:

100% TAILOR MADE
AUTHENTIC HEIRLOOM QUALITY
MADE FROM FAITH, FAMILY AND FRIENDS
HAND WASH ONLY WITH LOVE

When I look to God to help grant perspective, I marvel that we are given the gift of language. This memoir commenced with the magical language of a small child. In fact, we are constantly conjugating the verbs in life. Our sentence structure becomes more complex as does our living on this planet. All of us have begun with the "I" and perhaps shifted to the "Thou." As we accept ourselves as grown-up, we use the pronouns "him" and "her" and the "they" who inhabit this temporal, hurting world.

To learn how to speak a language requires an investment in listening and practicing. If you ask me to describe my religious preference, I would respond that I am, like the fabric of my life story, being mended, quilted, a Jew, a Baptist, a Presbyterian, and an Episcopalian.

I have practiced speaking the languages of growing up and independence, love and prayer, grief and counseling, trust and survival, and lastly, thankfulness and faith. I have been offered courage to speak the Language of Grace.